Fish Story
The Millers of Colfax

Scott Robey

ISBN: 1-4033-7076-1 (e-book)
ISBN: 1-4033-7077-X (Paperback)

Library of Congress Control Number: 2002094175

This book is printed on acid free paper.

Printed in the United States of America
Bloomington, IN

1stBooks – rev. 12/17/02

Contents

Dedicated in loving memory.

Ralph Ashley 6/6/1899—2/10/1980
Irene Ashley 6/12/1900—8/23/1998

Acknowledgements

I've never apologized for growing up on a farm at the edge of Colfax, Indiana—Colfax is my hometown. I must confess that during years of travel throughout the United States and Canada I was reluctant to tell people the specific place I was from. Reluctant not because I was ashamed of Colfax; I just assumed most people wouldn't know where it was and I would most likely end up explaining to people where my hometown was located in relationship to Indianapolis. When I offered the generic answer that I was from Indiana, I was often pressed to reveal the specific name of my hometown. When I divulged that it was Colfax I discovered just how many were asking for specifics because it was the one town in Indiana, other than Indianapolis, of which they were aware. In every case there was a reason why they knew of Colfax; they had been there and Miller's Restaurant had been the reason they were there.

Like many teenage boys growing up around Colfax, I did a tour of duty as a bus boy at Miller's. Any sixteen-year-old boy hired by Miller's discovered the meaning of hard work on his first weekend night of employment. I was a farm kid, but found myself thinking that a full day of baling hay was light work compared to an eight hour Saturday night shift at Miller's. Also, like most teenage boys, I was not cognizant of the significance of the events around me. I knew there were an immense number of people visiting Miller's during my years growing up, but at the time never pondered where the people might be coming from. Hearing that the customer count on a Purdue football Saturday had exceeded 1,200 people, I never translated it to mean that nearly twice the population of Colfax had passed through the doors of Miller's in a single eight-hour period.

Over the nearly thirty-five years since departing my boyhood home I've heard stories of Colfax and Miller's from local residents of San Diego, Minneapolis, Dallas, New Orleans, Miami and Toronto to name just a few. Only after experiencing these tales did it finally strike me just how much notoriety my hometown had gained over the years and what the source of this renown had been. These stories proved to be the initial impetus for writing the story of the Miller family of Colfax and the role they played in putting Colfax, Indiana on the map.

Some may know part of the story of Miller's, especially its final chapter; it's this last chapter that was the motivation for documenting the others. A burned-out building on the corner of what is now Main and Oakland Streets finally moved me to believe it was crucial that the story be documented of what had transpired in the building over the past fifty years. One day while standing on a street corner in Colfax I watched as James L. and Mary Ellen Miller passed by in a shiny convertible; they were participating in a Saturday morning parade that was part of Colfax's Hickory Days, a summer festival held in early August. The Millers were being honored by the festival organizers for having celebrated their 60th wedding anniversary just a few weeks before. As I watched the car pass by and then looked around at the crowd lining the street, it struck me that there was a dwindling number of people, even in Colfax, who actually knew who the Millers really were. Rather than being honored for 60 years of marriage, which is a noteworthy milestone, James and Mary Ellen Miller should have been honored for bringing a level of notoriety to Colfax that few towns of its size ever experience; this book is meant to rectify the oversight.

I'm proud to have grown up in Colfax. Of course, having so many people around the country acknowledge they knew of Colfax because of Miller's is one source of this pride; but for the most part, I'm proud of my hometown just because it was a good place to be during my time there. Parts of this story deal with the reality that Colfax has had a colorful and sometimes dubious past. It, like so many other small towns, has been populated throughout its history by a range of interesting and sometimes notorious characters who could be the subjects of a story all their own. Colfax had a unique collective personality before the Miller family came to town. Yet their arrival served to facilitate the discovery of the place I still refer to as my hometown by thousands of people.

Discovering sources for a story about Miller's Restaurant was not a challenge. The challenge lay in which of the hundreds (and probably more) of the stories should be included in the account of a legendary business. When approached about the possibility of a story about his life and business, James L. Miller first responded that he didn't have much of a story to tell; what follows proves he was being excessively modest. Once the process began he and his wife, Mary Ellen, discovered there was much to tell and they proved to be extremely candid in sharing the details of their lives. There are many stories of the struggle to start a business and to live out a dream documented on nearly 50 hours of taped interviews. The second generation of Millers, Mike and Beckie Miller, contributed greatly to the telling of the business' story from 1970 up to the time of its sale in 1995. The Millers are only part of the story; employees and legions of loyal customers played a significant role in defining Miller's Restaurant throughout its history.

What is written here is actually an amalgamation of dozens of recollections of Miller's. While an attempt is made to attribute comments to specific people, a portion of the narrative can only be classified as "a consensus opinion among many". A number of recollections are my own, accumulated over the nearly fifty years I've known the Miller family.

I'm grateful to a number of people for sharing their memories with me. When these people were contacted I expected only brief conversations about any thoughts they might have of Miller's. Most often brief conversations extended into hour-long reminiscences. I extend my thanks to Harry Bradway, Brad Blickenstaff, Betty Grim, Louise "Rio" Afflis, Gerald "Curley" Myers, Johnny Rutherford, the late Don Dixon, Jim Dixon, Kern Murray, Al and Betty Harding, Sal Fish (who did not change his name to be included in this story), Tom Cochrun, Linda Phebus, Andrea and Dwight Slipher, Cheri Cooper, Bob Higman, Todd McGraw, John Livengood, Reid Duffy and Rick Albrecht. Many current residents of Colfax contributed their recollections of Miller's and the town.

Former employees of Miller's Restaurant proved to be of immense value. Nancy Dowell, Suilon Benjamin, Bob Phebus (son of Meda Phebus), Mary Rominger, Velera Cain, Connie Pritchard, Dee Rhodes, Avis Davis, Maurice Cripe, Jr. (son of Beulah and Maurice "Pat" Cripe) and Alyne Hodges are all in my debt.

LeRoy Good provided useful information from his marvelous knowledge of Colfax and Clinton County. Thanks to Eric Smith, President of Results Communication Group in Frankfort for his assistance in scanning and preparing photography. Special recognition goes to Judy Hemmerling, Director of the Colfax Public Library and Phil White and the staff of the Genealogy Department at the Frankfort Community Library for their assistance and patience in my seemingly never-ending inquiries regarding source material. Linda Brammell, Clinton County Recorder, was a great help in leading me through the historical records that are so readily available to the public—I would have been lost without her assistance.

Most of all, I am thankful to, and for, my wife Susan. She displayed immense tolerance of the stacks of resource materials that were strewn about our house and willingly read numerous drafts of the manuscript. Most importantly, for some curious reason, she appears to still love me after all these years.

Everyone who contributed to this work seemed to sense they were not only contributing to a biography but to a love story. I hope that for many people it will prove to be both.

Scott Robey
Lafayette, IN

A note of caution:

For those who were frequent customers of Miller's Restaurant, reading the balance of this book may cause overwhelming cravings for fried catfish and onion rings that might be impossible to satisfy. No responsibility is assumed for this condition. Proceed at your own risk.

Introduction

The catfish is a plenty good enough fish for anyone.
—Mark Twain

A man ambled along Colfax's Oakland Street toward the center of town. He needn't be closer than two blocks from view for anyone to know who was approaching in the late afternoon sunlight. A powerful hulk of a man— always walking with his shoulders hunched slightly forward, he was dressed in a bright white uniform so heavily starched one wondered how the man could move at all. But it was the uniform he'd worn almost every afternoon for nearly fifty years. Most afternoons he walked at a brisk pace, an energetic gait of someone who was about to go on stage to perform and most who knew him considered him a virtuoso performer. But this late afternoon of April 15, 1995, his stride was shorter, slower. He had tried for days to not dwell on this afternoon's stroll—the last he would ever take as the owner of Miller's Restaurant.

James L. Miller and his son and co-owner, Mike, had made the decision that their business of nearly fifty years should be sold. This afternoon was the beginning of the last day the Miller family was to own a business that had defined their lives and the reputation of the small farm town of Colfax, Indiana. It was a difficult decision, but one that had to be made. Even when the details of the sale were being worked out, it didn't really register that this last walk would be only a few weeks away. James L. Miller paused in front of Wright's Hardware Store at the corner of Oakland and Franklin to peer across the street and take one last panoramic view of his business—a business that would belong to someone else on Monday. It took only seconds to distill the memories that had accumulated since the late October evening in 1946 when he first showed his young wife, Mary Ellen, what was to be their new livelihood. He allowed a faint smile to spread across his face when he remembered her reaction to the smoke-filled beer hall and the shocking event that had unfolded as they pulled up to the side of the building. Yet, just as she had done in the first years of their marriage, she followed him toward his dream, a dream that came true in the little town of Colfax.

The town of Colfax, Indiana has a land area of one-third square mile, about two hundred and twelve acres and has never been populated by more than 850 citizens at any time in its history. For those wondering what Colfax might be close to, the answer is simple: the only place it's close to is the ground. The state capitol of Indianapolis is forty miles away (as the crow flies) and Lafayette is nearly twenty miles to the northwest. If the retail mantra of "location, location, location" is true, then the story of Miller's Restaurant becomes quite implausible.

The story of Miller's begins when a young man buys a business that had been nothing more than a raucous beer joint that would have fit comfortably in a scene from the Old West. Through a combination of excruciating hard work, experimentation, and some luck, Miller's grew to become one of the most famous dining establishments in the history of Indiana. What follows is the story of Miller's Restaurant and how it built its reputation throughout the United States and several foreign countries. While there are a number of restaurants throughout Indiana that have enjoyed wide-spread recognition in Indiana and the Midwest, few can claim the nationwide reputation that Miller's built during its nearly fifty years of ownership by the Miller family of Colfax.

The story of Miller's Restaurant is more than just a story of good food and service; it's a story of a community—a community that was, early on, uncertain it wanted this young couple and, what was then, their tavern. Not many years passed before the community discovered it was becoming as famous as the fish suppers being served at the corner of Railroad and Oakland streets.

While many small towns spend their days in quiet obscurity, Colfax was far from obscure. In the period spanning October 1946 to April 1995, nearly five million people found their way to Colfax and over fifteen million catfish sacrificed their lives to satisfy the cravings of those who made the trip. This fish story is, in the parlance of the town liar's bench, a real "whopper"; the only difference is—this "whopper" is true.

Colfax, Indiana. 1913. View looking west along Railroad Street. The Miller's building can be seen on the right at the southeast corner of the intersection. The steeple of the St. George Catholic Church can be seen at the far end of the street.

Scott Robey

Chapter One

Gunfire on a Saturday night.

As he guided his 1939 DeSoto along a lonely county road, Ralph Ashley glanced at the young man sitting on the passenger seat next to him in the car's dark interior. It was Saturday, October 19, 1946 and he wondered what his twenty-seven year son-in-law was about to get himself into. He worried more about his daughter, Mary Ellen, who sat next to her mother, Irene, in the back seat of the jet-black automobile. The young man, James L. Miller, sat in silence staring out at the dimly lit road; he too wondered what his future held. Regardless of any doubts he harbored, he had assured his twenty-three year old wife that a bright future would be theirs in the tiny town of Colfax, Indiana.

As the old DeSoto reached the two lanes of State Road 52, James Miller knew he was only five minutes from introducing his wife to his newly acquired source of livelihood. After their marriage, Mary Ellen Miller had followed her husband around the country from Army base to base before he was sent overseas in the last year of the World War. Now, only ten months since his return from the war, he hoped she would be as willing to follow him the twelve miles to his new adventure. Coming into Colfax as the county road morphed into what came to be known as Old Main Street, they turned north on Columbia Street and traveled parallel to the railroad running along the eastern perimeter of town. When Ralph Ashley came to the intersection of Columbia and Railroad Streets, with the train depot and hotel on the right, James Miller motioned for his father-in-law to turn left onto Railroad Street. After traveling a block, Ralph Ashley turned onto Oakland Street and guided his DeSoto into a parking spot adjacent to the post office.

The four sat in silence, staring across at a corner building. Light created a hazy aura on the adjacent sidewalk as it struggled to escape through the grimy windows. As they gazed at the establishment, the door at the front of the building burst open—a man raced from the building, slamming the door behind him. The door had barely closed before it exploded open again and a second man stormed from the building. The second man took two steps from the door, turned, stopped and reached into his coat pocket. The four occupants of Ralph Ashley's DeSoto were unsure what the man had pulled from his pocket—uncertain until the man extended his right arm and fired at the man who had fled down the dark sidewalk. The gunman dropped his arm to his side and stared down the sidewalk into the darkness of the cold night. After a few seconds, he slid the gun into his jacket pocket and disappeared back into the noisy building. James Miller had gotten his first real glimpse of his new business—he had been told it was a real "Saturday night kind of joint"; a beer joint where it appeared disputes were not settled with diplomacy, but with various caliber handguns.

James Miller stared out through the car's windshield; he was reluctant to turn to see the expression on his wife's face in the darkness of the car's interior. He was afraid that if he turned to face his wife, she might insist they leave Colfax forever. The four sat in silence for what seemed—at least to James Miller—an eternity; Ralph Ashley finally broke the silence. Opening the driver's side door, he turned to his son-in-law, "I guess we should go in and take a look around." The two women remained silent in the back seat. Ralph and James exited the car and stood in the street, waiting for the two women to join them; James Miller was not sure whether his wife would get out of the car. Finally, the back, street-side door of the car opened and the two women slid from the seat. James Miller saw his young wife's eyes were fixed on the front door where the gunman had rushed out. More disconcerting was that the man had reentered the building the four visitors were about to inspect.

The four crossed the street and entered the building through a side door. Brooks' Restaurant was a misnomer of sorts. It was more saloon than restaurant, primarily serving sandwiches that were prepared by slicing off chunks of ham and roast beef that sat in the open on the back bar—a practice that would horrify a modern day health inspector. As the four entered the back door of the "restaurant" a small, homely man met them. The most striking feature of the man Mary Ellen Miller noticed was that his hands were covered in motor grease and grime. She first thought the man was assigned the job of waiting on the four tables that sat to the rear of the main bar area; actually, the little man was employed to do janitorial chores and stack beer cases in the rear of the establishment.

James Miller led his companions through a cramped kitchen and into the small dining area. The establishment was so small that the four had to only move a few steps from the back kitchen to survey the entire business. A thick haze of smoke hung from the ceiling of the barroom, making it difficult to see the faces of the more than two- dozen patrons who stood, swilling beer and talking in near shouts. Mary Ellen Miller studied the crowd intently, attempting to identify the man who, just minutes before, had fired a gun into the darkness. With the memory of the gunshot in her mind, she was keenly aware that at least one man in the noisy crowd was carrying a firearm—she was certain there were others.

Mary Ellen Miller, only slightly more than five feet tall and normally soft-spoken, turned to her husband and tersely asked, "What in the hell have you got me into?" James Miller stared intently into the smoke filled barroom without responding—or looking directly at his wife; he couldn't— the knot in his stomach was making it difficult to speak. Years later he

7

would comment, "I knew the place would be a challenge, but I desperately wanted a place of my own and here it was. I was used to cleaning places up and I figured I could do it here."

James Miller thought his wife and in-laws had seen enough. Ralph Ashley, trying to put a positive spin on the situation, said he thought the place looked pretty good; the women didn't seem to be in as complimentary a mood. James guided his companions out the back door toward the car, hoping all the time that gunfire would not ring out again before they could leave town. James led his wife to the car, opened the door to the back seat of the DeSoto and, noticing that she had continued to stare at the front door of the restaurant as she crossed the street, helped her slide onto the seat. Before he closed the door, Mary Ellen Miller looked up to her husband and said, "You still didn't answer my question." He hadn't answered the question because he wasn't sure he had a good answer at the moment. James Miller was unsure whether his wife would ever return to Colfax again.

Less than forty-eight hours elapsed before the four traveled the same road to Colfax—this time following a neighbor's truck that had been loaded with James and Mary Ellen Miller's furniture and other household belongings. The truck and the DeSoto pulled up to the Oakland Street side of Brooks' Restaurant that had become their property earlier in the day. Mary Ellen Miller thought the establishment to be more appealing in the quiet hours of the sunlit morning, the bright white exterior of the building actually looked inviting from the street, especially since they had sat alongside the building for nearly five minutes and no gunfire had erupted. The October 24, 1946 edition of the *Clinton County Review*, a weekly newspaper published in Colfax, reported the incident. Winifred Davis was charged with carrying a concealed 32-caliber pistol and discharging it at his brother-in-law, Robert Tyre, who was charged with disorderly conduct; both men pleaded not guilty to the charges.

Miller's Restaurant was not only going to be James and Mary Ellen's livelihood, but also their new home. From the early 1900's until 1936, the building had housed one of Colfax's two hotels and a five-room apartment had been fashioned from the rooms on the second floor of the building. Ralph Ashley and his son-in-law lugged the Miller's belongings into the dining area of the restaurant and up the narrow, winding stairs to the apartment. After arranging the four pieces of furniture that had been purchased shortly after their marriage and, unpacking the few boxes containing the remainder of their household goods, James and Mary Ellen prepared to open for business as the new owners of Colfax's only bar and grill—Brooks' Restaurant would open up the next day as Miller's Restaurant.

Brooks' Restaurant was never in danger of being mistaken for a fine dining establishment. Its primary attraction was a well-stocked cooler of cold, fifteen-cent beer. The kitchen in the rear of the business had a grill that often went unused during business hours. The steady clientele proved to be mostly the crowd Mary Ellen Miller had observed on the Saturday night she was first introduced to her husband's new business venture. The nightly customer base was comprised of farmers and workers from the local furniture factory, the Indiana Hickory Furniture Company. The company, started by J. C. Jordan in an old tile factory, manufactured hickory desks and other furniture and promoted itself as "The Home of Handsome Hickory". The crowds also included members of road construction gangs who were beginning work on expanding State Road 52 from two to four lanes, when it would become designated as a U.S. highway. The remaining customers were men whose only avocation appeared to be drinking large amounts of beer. Problems were cropping up from the friction between locals and an out-of-town crowd that had started to frequent Brooks' Restaurant. The only tavern in nearby Thorntown had closed, prompting its former customers to make the eight-mile trip to Colfax. The "Bucktowners" didn't always see eye-to-eye with the Colfax crowd, creating an atmosphere that had potential for more gunplay.

Like many young men who dream of their own business and find themselves presented with the opportunity, James Miller had rushed to judgment; he had not examined the premises as thoroughly as he should have. While the grimy tavern was something he felt he could clean up, he had not inspected the entire facility prior to its purchase, an inspection that would have uncovered the building's other inhabitants. Within a few days of taking over the restaurant, an early November chill came to town revealing a malfunctioning furnace that was housed in the basement of the building. After James Miller descended the rickety stairs to the basement, he realized his new business was home to the largest population of rats this side of Calcutta. The rats had found ample food supplies in the garbage cans sitting at the rear of the restaurant and, if the garbage ran low, James found they could have survived by consuming the armies of cockroaches that ran freely about the place. After using a broom to break up the assemblage of rats huddled near the furnace, he was able to get the furnace operating. James sensed the rats were pleased that the heat that usually emanated from the furnace would soon return. He turned and walked toward the stairs that led to the first floor to discover a large rat, about the size of a small cat, perched squarely at eye level on the fifth step. The rat, having reared up on its hind legs, appeared to be challenging James' exit from the basement. A mighty swat with a coal shovel reduced the rat population by one, but James knew he couldn't win his personal rat race one rat at a time and certainly not one cockroach at a time. His next call was to a Frankfort exterminator who, after examining the premises, joked that he would have to call for backup to complete the job.

James Miller had a clear vision of what his place was to become and the vision did not include legions of rats, cockroaches or a number of his current customers. He knew that over time, he could clean up his new restaurant, including a thorough scrubbing of the oiled wood floor, but his decision to clean up the clientele would be much more difficult. After only a few nights of mopping up huge puddles of tobacco juice and large wads of gnarled tobacco plugs that had been discarded on the floor by beer guzzling patrons, he arrived at the difficult decision that it was time to make a change. He had already expelled the majority of the Thorntown crowd and over the course of the next month he informed another twenty customers they were no longer welcome in Miller's Restaurant. It was a decision that carried significant financial consequences. Each of the banned customers was consuming as much as a dollar's worth of beer every night; the removal of twenty customers represented a loss of over a hundred dollars of revenue each week. The five thousand dollars of lost annual sales would be significant for a business that had been projected to earn only a thousand dollars of net profit in its first year.

James Miller was not making value judgments when he banished his unruly patrons from the business, he was simply making a business decision. The new owner of Miller's Restaurant realized that if he didn't make a change in his clientele, his business would remain as it was—a beer joint. Over thirty years later he would tell Myrtie Barker, who was interviewing him on behalf of the *Indianapolis News*, that he knew there "had to be more to life than picking drunks up off the floor." He knew it would never evolve into the kind of restaurant he'd dreamed of owning—the cussers and the spitters had to go. Several of the exiled accused him of running a "Sunday School class". James Miller quickly retorted that if that's what they thought, it meant he was on his way to where he wanted to be. He began paying Raleigh Higer, the Colfax town marshal, five dollars a night to sit in the bar on Saturday nights to ensure the banished stayed out. Higer was noted for his ability to keep the peace, having once arrested his own brother while serving as the town's marshal.

Over the next few months the rats and cockroaches disappeared and so did the riffraff. The Millers were enjoying their new apartment atop the restaurant. Upon James' return from the Army, the two had lived in a shoebox-sized trailer parked in the Ashley's back yard; the fact that the apartment had a bathroom seemed a luxury. Business was good and neither minded the eighteen hour days that were now their way of life, a life Mary Ellen Miller could not possibly have envisioned six years before on the day, sitting under an old willow tree, she had said "yes" to the most important question of her life.

Mary Ellen and James L. Miller. June 29, 1941

Chapter Two

When Mary met Jerry.

Mary Ellen Ashley accepted a marriage proposal from a man who was using an assumed name. It wasn't that the man was intentionally deceiving her, but he had developed an identity crisis because everyone but him had played a role in assigning him the name by which he would be known. A discussion of his real name had not come up during their courtship and when, under a willow tree on Frankfort's First Street the man had asked her to marry him, Mary Ellen told Jerry Miller she accepted his proposal.

James Levi Miller was born February 2, 1919, the son of James Oscar Miller and the former Anna May Shaff. At the time of James L. Miller's birth, the family lived south of Frankfort on the Kirklin Brick road, a road where James O. Miller had worked to lay the brick. James L. Miller was given the middle name, Levi as a tribute to his grandfather, Levi Miller. The last-born of the Miller's four sons, James was assigned the moniker of Junior early in his life—he was the youngest and carried the name of both his father and grandfather. According to James L. Miller, "Jr. got tacked on when I was a child and, for the most part, never left me. Believe me I tried to get rid of it when I was young, but I wasn't able to do it."

Before James L. reached his second birthday his family moved from the Kirklin Brick to a house that occupied a tract of land at 305 S. Williams Street in Frankfort. Shortly after moving into the house, the family learned the property facing Williams Street had been acquired by the local school board for the construction of the Riley Elementary School. In order to make room for the school, the Miller house was lifted, placed on large rollers and moved to the east end of Boone Street. The Miller family continued to occupy the house as it was being moved. The house, owned by the F.C.

Coulter estate, was placed on a large foundation and basement that was located on property also owned by the estate; the lot lay along the eastern-most edge of Frankfort's city limits. Coulter had built a large dairy barn just to the east of the house that sat outside the city limit. James O. Miller leased the farm and dairy barn from the Coulter estate and began milking cows. He and his wife processed the milk in the large basement of their house and developed a route of steady customers for their milk, butter and cheese, making home deliveries in an old Model T Ford. Jr. Miller remembers, "My parents made a living a nickel at a time, but we did OK; we always had something to eat."

After seven years in the dairy business, James O. Miller grew weary of the seven days a week routine and moved his family three miles east of Frankfort to the L. M. Morris farm. Jr. Miller had completed the fourth grade at Riley Elementary, which had opened in the fall of 1923, when his father again pulled up roots and moved north of Frankfort to the Humes farm where Jr. was enrolled at the Scroggy School. In the summer of 1931, James O. Miller fell ill and found himself unable to handle the 125-acre Humes farm. The Miller family moved to Maple Lodge, a small farm north of Jefferson, Indiana where Jr. completed his seventh year of school. James O. Miller's health continued to deteriorate and he died on September 14, 1932. In the depths of the Depression, Anna May Miller was left with three sons still living at home. She made the decision to send her youngest son to live with a distant cousin and he again found himself enrolled for his eighth school year at the Scroggy School. To support her family, Anna May Miller began working as a practical nurse after moving to a house on Washington Avenue in Frankfort. James L. Miller, now called Jr. by most, completed his last year at Scroggy and moved back with his mother where he would attend Frankfort High School.

Jr. Miller attended Frankfort High School where he was an above average student. He was able to contribute to his family's income working for his oldest brother, Ellsworth, who was the daytime manager of Wheeler's Restaurant at the corner of Washington and Jackson Streets. Jr. would come to Wheeler's during his school lunch break and earn his lunch by washing lunch crowd dishes, finishing his work in time to return for his afternoon classes. He'd return to work the night shift as a dishwasher at Wheeler's where his brother, Norman, was the night manager; Norman Miller paid his younger brother 20 cents an hour. Jr. continued to work for Ellsworth Miller after he purchased the Sanitary Waffle Shop located at Eight W. Washington Street. On July 27, 1936, prior to Jr.'s senior year at Frankfort High School, Anna May Miller died in the Frankfort hospital from complications following surgery. Jr. moved in with his brother Herb, who now lived on Frankfort's West Armstrong Street.

Mary Ellen Ashley was born in Indianapolis on March 13, 1923, the daughter of Ralph and Irene Ashley. Ralph Ashley, who had been born in Frankfort, moved to Indianapolis after World War I to work for an outdoor advertising company. He met and married Irene Meikel and, shortly after their marriage, he took over a delivery route for a bottled water company. The Ashleys moved to Frankfort in 1926 when Ralph took a job as a switchman with the Nickel Plate Railroad. While they first lived on Frankfort's Hoke Avenue, they moved to 1400 Washington Street two years later, and then across the street to 1401 in 1930. Mary Ellen Ashley's brother, Frank, was born in 1921. Staff Sergeant Frank Ashley was killed on June 16, 1944 while serving with the 15th Air Force as a B-24 tail gunner during a mission over Austria. He was interred in France's Lorraine American Cemetery and Memorial. Mary Ellen Ashley's sister, Barbara, was born in 1932 and spent most of her life in California.

Because of the four-year difference in their ages, Mary Ellen Ashley never met James. L. "Jr." Miller while he was a student at Frankfort High School; that changed in 1939. The Ashley's paperboy, Don Foster, had taken an interest in Mary Ellen while she was a student at Riley Elementary, an interest that was not reciprocated by her because Foster was two years older than she. Jr. was in high school and had developed an interest in an attractive classmate who told him she would never accept a date if he went by the name of Jr. She took it upon herself to begin calling Jr. Miller— Jerry. Consequently, the girl had introduced her friend Don Foster to Jr. Miller as Jerry Miller.

By the time Mary Ellen entered high school, Don Foster's interest in her had intensified. As young boys often do, he kept talking about his good friend Jerry Miller. He would go on about how smart Jerry Miller was and how handsome he was. Mary Ellen Ashley had no interest in Jerry Miller and only slightly more interest in Don Foster. "I got so tired of hearing about this Jerry Miller character," Mary Ellen said, "I finally told my mother that I'd do a turnaround on Don and tell him how good looking I thought this Jerry was and how I'd really like to meet him. Don told me I'd have to wait until Christmas."

The telephone rang as the Ashleys were having dinner on Christmas day, 1939. Ralph Ashley answered the telephone and told his son the call was for him. Frank returned to the table and, attempting to disguise a smile, told the family the call had been from Don Foster, but that he had had nothing important to say. Shortly after dinner, Frank invited his sister to take a drive around town. While they were out, Mary Ellen told her brother that she knew what was going on. She knew that Don Foster had told Frank to get her out of the house while he brought Jerry Miller over. She reiterated to her brother that she had no real interest in meeting Jerry Miller.

What she didn't know was how grand an entrance the two young men had planned.

Jerry Miller, who had graduated from high school the previous May, had never met any of Mary Ellen Ashley's family. Consequently, it made what Mary Ellen was about to witness even more memorable. Don Foster did bring Jerry Miller over to the Ashley house, not to sit on the couch waiting for Mary Ellen, but under the Christmas tree. Foster had hand-lettered a ribbon that read "Jerry to Mary Ellen, From Don. Merry Christmas" and draped it across his friend's chest. He also coached his friend on what to do when Mary Ellen entered the room. Jerry Miller was initially reticent to be so theatrical in front of adults he had known for less than ten minutes, but decided to follow his friend's directions. When Mary Ellen entered the room, Jerry Miller leapt to his feet and shouted, "Darling I'm here." Mary Ellen Miller still has the hand-lettered ribbon stored in a cedar chest.

Shortly after Christmas, Mary Ellen Ashley conspired to make Don Foster jealous by accepting Jerry Miller's invitation for a date. Several dates with Jerry ensued during the spring of her junior year at Frankfort High School. After the completion of the school year, Mary Ellen traveled to California in the summer of 1940 to spend the summer with her aunt. It proved to be an eventful trip when she met the actor Errol Flynn at the Hotel Coronado in San Diego. When she arrived back in Chicago in August she was met by her parents and, Jerry Miller.

The fact that Mary Ellen met Jerry Miller was, in itself, an act of fate. After graduating from Frankfort High School in 1938, he developed a case of wanderlust. Still living with his brother Herb, he made the decision to see the country. Herb Miller drove his brother to the south edge of Frankfort and Jerry Miller set off to hitch hike across America. After an overnight stay in St. Louis, he reached Jefferson City, Missouri, and had run out of money. He took a job in a grimy hash house as a dishwasher until he'd earned enough money to continue his trek across the country. Again, out of money, he stopped long enough in Kansas City to take a job working at a small diner in the commercial fruit market section of the city; he continued on to Denver in only a few days.

Upon his arrival in Denver he visited the local employment security office and was given a job lead at the Brooks' Forest Summer Resort in Evergreen, Colorado; the name of the resort later turned out to be an interesting coincidence. When he appeared at the resort in person, he was immediately hired as a dishwasher for a weekly salary of $5.00 plus room and board. He was expected to serve meals to the other help as part of his dishwasher's job where he demonstrated a talent for balancing a number of plates up his arm. When the headwaiter was fired, the manager of the resort made the young Hoosier a dining room waiter.

Waiters at the resort were expected to wear alpine-style uniforms, including short leather pants. During his time waiting tables, the handsome young man attracted the attention of actress Fay Holden, who often played the role of Mickey Rooney's mother in the Andy Hardy films. Any time he found himself close to Ms. Holden's table, he had to contend with the 43-year-old actress secretly fondling his leg.

Had Jerry Miller become enamored with the Rocky Mountains he might have never returned to Frankfort. However, it took less than six weeks for homesickness to take hold of the young man from the Clinton County farm country. He returned to Frankfort and took a job with a food service company in Lebanon, Indiana that toured with a carnival. Jerry found himself traveling to Columbus, Ohio and then back to Indianapolis for the Indiana State Fair. From there, the carnival hit the road again for Louisville,

Kentucky, parts of Tennessee, and then on into North Carolina. During the carnival's stay in North Carolina Jerry arrived late for work after a late night drinking binge with a fellow carney; his tardiness and physical condition led to his dismissal. He had just enough money left from his last paycheck to buy a bus ticket back to Frankfort. Having spent his last few cents on bus fare, he found himself introduced to the concept of pay toilets in the Columbus, Ohio bus station. He recollects that the squeeze under the door of the toilet was difficult for a young man his size.

Upon his return from North Carolina, Jerry took a job laying sod along State Road 52 for 60 cents an hour and then, a few weeks later, he went to work for Franklin Hart. Hart owned restaurants in Lebanon and Logansport, Indiana, and had purchased the Sanitary Waffle Shop when Ellsworth Miller made the decision to sell his business. It had not been Ellsworth Miller's decision, but his wife's. Ellsworth had made a habit of participating in the high stakes poker games around Frankfort and she demanded he sell the business. They relocated to Goshen, Indiana where Ellsworth took a job at the Hamilton Steel Works plant, owned by his father-in-law. Norman Miller was to later move to Goshen where he owned and operated a number of successful businesses. Jerry Miller worked in all three Hart's Restaurants, going from town to town where he was needed for the day, usually to fill in whenever a grill cook had quit. "I didn't care where I went. I just worked because I had to. I'd spent $45 for an engagement ring in Logansport and had to pay a dollar a week to pay it off."

Just two weeks after Mary Ellen Ashley's return from California, she and Jerry rode bicycles to Don Foster's parent's house on First Street (they had dated on bicycles before Mary Ellen's trip to California). After leading Mary Ellen over to a large willow tree in the backyard, Jerry Miller knelt down, removed the recently purchased engagement ring from his pocket, and asked her to marry him. During the short time they had dated, Mary Ellen Ashley had found that Don Foster had been right in his assessment of his friend Jerry. He was handsome—he was smart—and, she had fallen in love with him. Mary Ellen Ashley told Jerry Miller she would marry him. There is some dispute between husband and wife as to whether Jerry was on his knees when he proposed. Mary Ellen Ashley spent her senior year in high school sporting the ring her fiancée would pay off over the next forty-five weeks.

Mary Ellen Ashley and Jerry Miller were to be married on June 29, 1941. They found an apartment at 1351 N. Main Street in Frankfort and decided the wedding would be held there, with the Reverend Stephan P. O'Reilley of the United Brethren Church officiating. Mrs. Anna Barton, widow of John Barton, was the Miller's landlady. She contributed to the wedding plans by pledging to provide a generous supply of her homemade cherry wine. The apartment was spacious for a young couple: a living room, bedroom, bathroom, and a kitchen with refrigerator and work table; and a small side porch was roomy enough for a dining table.

The couple went to the Clinton County courthouse for their marriage license and after the license was issued, Mary Ellen examined it to discover that the man she was about to marry, Jerry Miller, was actually James Levi Miller. James—Jerry—Jr. attempted to explain the evolution of his many names, passing lightly over the fact that a former girl friend had actually christened him Jerry. Mary Ellen Ashley understood his true given name and the fact he was the youngest son and bore the name of both his father and grandfather. However, she wasn't as understanding of Jerry, indicating that Jr. had not passed over its source lightly enough. Nevertheless, the wedding plans were not affected. Mary Ellen Ashley was relieved she'd actually know her new husband's real name before the vows had been completed; she would spend the rest of her life with a man called "Jr.".

Frank Ashley was Jr. Miller's best man and Mary Ellen's high school friend, Louise Baker, served as Maid of Honor. The bride entered on her father's arm from the bedroom and stopped at an arched entryway into the apartment's living room. Irene Ashley was stationed in the kitchen, attending to a Victrola® that played *I Love You Truly.* She rewound the player several times as the song played over and over throughout the ceremony. Ralph Ashley played a role beyond being father of the bride by also baking the couple's wedding cake and providing the flowers for the ceremony. Mary Ellen Miller estimates her father purchased at least two-dozen gladioli—nearly $3.00 worth of flowers at the time. At 2:30 p.m. on June 29, 1941, under the curved archway between an apartment bedroom and living room, James L. Miller and Mary Ellen Ashley became husband and wife.

After briefly celebrating with the ceremony's attendees, cutting Ralph Ashley's wedding cake and toasting to a long, happy marriage, the couple headed to Indianapolis for their honeymoon. Since Jr. didn't own an automobile, Ralph Ashley served as chauffeur to the Washington Hotel. The Miller's honeymooned for less than 24 hours. Jr. had taken a new job as a cook at the Frankfort Elk's Club and he felt he couldn't miss work, especially since he was now making $25 a week. The two returned to Frankfort on a bus the morning after their wedding.

Jr. Miller worked at the Elk's Club until his induction into the Army on May 19, 1942 when he was sent to Fort Hamilton, New York earning $21.00 a month. While he'd never held a rifle in his life and was not completely familiar with the difference between his right and left foot, he discovered that the first few weeks of the military were all about discipline;

entire days were spent drilling on a football field outside the fort. In October 1942, he shipped out to Fort Patrick Henry in Newport News, Virginia, a base that was to be used later in the war as an internment camp for German POWs. Upon arrival at Patrick Henry, he was assigned the task of running the mess hall. He didn't realize at the time that the challenge of a mess hall the size of Patrick Henry's would make serving 1,000 catfish dinners on a Saturday night seem relatively easy. Because of the number of trainees arriving at Patrick Henry, it was not uncommon for the mess to sometimes feed 5,000 men at each meal—15,000 meals a day. Jr. went into the service as a PFC, but was promoted to Mess Sergeant without ever having done any cooking beyond short order grillwork. He had never pulled KP, but because, as he says, "I answered the right questions," he was put in charge of the mess. The mess hall had 14 cook stoves, four 60-gallon fryers, ovens for baking and several huge steamers. In his previous cooking experience he had not discovered that a potato could be cooked any other way than boiling it.

He had a cadre of 23 men and depended on incoming troops to serve as cooks, KPs, bakers, and butchers. He was fortunate to have a cook who had served as a chef at a large New York hotel. The only flaw with the cook was that he was an alcoholic and would make up large batches of Apple Jack from the old fruit in the mess hall kitchen. The cook would hide each batch in the cook stoves when they weren't being used. The former chef's secret was discovered one day when a new shipment of troops arrived and the idle cook stoves were turned on without realizing the cook's stash was inside. It was nearly two days before troops could eat a meal without getting punch drunk from the fumes that wafted through the kitchen and mess hall.

Mary Ellen Miller soon joined her husband at Patrick Henry; she had worked three months at Milner's Packing House in Frankfort before making the trip to Virginia. She took a job in Newport News as a telephone operator, but found it didn't allow her to see her husband as often as she wanted. Answering a newspaper ad seeking workers for the Patrick Henry PX, she was hired and assigned to the PX in Area Eight of the fort, the same area where Jr.'s mess hall was located. In the beginning, she would ride an old Army truck to the fort before a bus route was finally established. She was willing to make the trip any way possible to see her husband every day. Shortly after taking the PX job, she was promoted to the assistant manager's position. While she enjoyed the work, it also provided a traumatic glimpse into the horrors of war—a war her husband might be called into at any time. Many of the young recruits had begun to rely on Mary Ellen for advice on gifts for their mothers, girl friends and wives. They would often give her money and she would pick out a gift from the PX jewelry counter, wrap it and send it on. One group of young commandos made a special effort to stop by the PX just before being shipped out—they wanted to thank her for her help and friendship. Word came back to the fort ten days later that the entire group had been killed en route to their destination when the Germans attacked their troop carrier.

Mary Ellen Miller was aware of the Federal Bureau of Investigation only because of the publicity it had received in its pursuit of one of Indiana's most notorious criminals, John Dillinger. It was not until a summer morning in 1943 she realized the FBI was aware of her. An agent contacted Mary Ellen Miller asking to meet her. Assuming she was in no position to decline the request, when the meeting took place, the agent removed a folder from his grip. Laying it out in front of her, she saw the FBI had assembled a complete dossier of her life. The agent explained they had done a background check on her because they wanted her to become a contact inside the Area Eight PX. She was to report any suspicious activity around the PX and, if she became suspicious of anyone, she was to contact the FBI immediately. The FBI's background check had indicated she would be a reliable source for such a surveillance project. Within a few days, Mary Ellen was entering the PX with her government identification badge pinned to her blouse and her FBI identification hidden in her shoe. The FBI tested her by sending a man into the PX dressed as a German soldier—Mary Ellen passed the test by contacting the agency immediately. The real stress of the assignment came with Jr.'s growing suspicion of the confidential letters she received on a weekly basis; he wondered if Mary Ellen had developed a personal relationship with one of her PX customers.

After a year and a half, the Army began assigning "casuals" to assist in the mess area. Jr. had already established a no-nonsense approach to preparing food and the casuals lacked the discipline he'd grown accustomed to with incoming troops serving in his mess operation. A number of run-ins with the casuals led to his being threatened several times with physical attack. The threats moved him to ponder what his options in the Army might be. One day as he was walking into the mess, he spotted a poster that had been tacked up in the entryway; the poster announced "The Infantry Wants You". He now held the rank of Platoon Sergeant and he made up his mind that, "If I was going to be killed it was going to be in the service of my country and not walking back to my barracks some night." Jr. informed Mary Ellen of his intentions and, as in later years, she supported his decision. He signed up and, in less than a week, the call came for him to join the infantry. He was sent to Camp Shelby, ten miles south of Hattiesburg, Mississippi, where he was assigned to a battalion with the rank of Platoon Sergeant. Since the couple had determined Jr. would only be at

Camp Shelby for a short time before being assigned duty overseas, Mary Ellen decided to stay at Patrick Henry. She had been moved to the fort's hospital PX as manager—she also had been able to shed the trying assignment of working undercover for the FBI.

Jr. was taught platoon tactics and earned expert rifleman status, the only Platoon Sergeant in the company to earn such recognition. The fact that this "Mess Sergeant" had out-gunned all other Platoon Sergeants earned the remaining men a tirade from the company commander; two were eventually busted in rank.

Jr. realized in just a matter of days that he sorely missed his young wife. He sent an SOS to her, asking that she come to Hattiesburg. Mary Ellen resisted the move at first, rationalizing that Jr. wasn't going to be at Camp Shelby that long and, most importantly, she was earning good money—considerably better than her husband's Army wages. She was sending a portion of her weekly salary home to her parents so they could make payments on the furniture the couple had purchased the week they were married. Jr. finally convinced Mary Ellen to leave Virginia; she arrived in Hattiesburg in early November 1944. After a few weeks, boredom led her to seek employment. Jr. was engaging in maneuvers nearly every night and could not leave the base to see his wife. She was unsuccessful at finding a job, which she later discovered would have provided money for her journey back to Frankfort.

Jr. had developed a friendship with fellow Hoosier, Roy Williams. Williams' wife, Dorothy, and infant daughter had come to Hattiesburg to join him. When Jr. and Roy Williams received their orders to ship to Camp Shanks, New York to prepare for departure overseas, Roy told the women they should return to Indiana. They set off in the Williams' old car, heading toward Indianapolis, Dorothy Williams' hometown. Having very little money, the women and the eighteen-month-old child, Carol Dee, slept in the car the first night of the trip. On the second day they experienced car trouble but fortunately were able to spend the night with a local farmer while the car was repaired, appreciating the warm beds, but relishing even more the ample hot meal the farmer's wife provided. They set off again and, upon reaching Southern Illinois, decided they should stay in a motel for the night. They crawled around on the car floor, scavenging enough spare change to pay for a night's lodging and a small bottle of milk for Carol Dee. Money was not the only issue. The women were within a hundred miles of Indianapolis but, because of gas rationing, were not sure they had sufficient coupons to purchase gasoline for the remainder of the trip. They arrived in Indianapolis with a gallon of gas in the car's tank and seven cents in their pockets.

Dorothy Williams' mother loaned Mary Ellen enough money to pay for a bus ticket back to Frankfort. Shortly after her return, she received a call from Jr. telling her that he'd received his orders to go overseas. He was shipped to LeHarve, France, arriving on January 21, 1945 as a member of the 261st Infantry Regiment, 65th Division. His regiment had been scheduled to arrive in England, but the urgent situation following the Battle of the Bulge necessitated being sent directly to France. Upon his return to the United States in January 1946, Jr. told his wife and friends that he felt fortunate to have participated in the conflict, even though it had been in its later stages; he had been privileged to be addressed by General George Patton who told those assembled they should be proud to be at the front, they had done something they could tell their grandchildren.

During the time Jr. was in Europe, Mary Ellen had taken a job as a "service girl" with Eli Lilly & Company after a short-lived job at the Hook's Drugstore in Frankfort. Living in a women's hotel on Indianapolis'

Delaware Street, she proved to be a valued employee. Wanting Mary Ellen to remain with the company, her supervisors pressed her for what her plans would be after her husband returned from the war. She and Jr. talked about the possibility that he might remain in the service; he had been a good soldier and he seriously considered making the Army a career. His early years of hitchhiking to Colorado and then traveling with the carnival had proved he was flexible enough to contend with the vagabond life of a career Army man. After experiencing the trip from Hattiesburg to Indiana, his wife was not so sure she could be as flexible. After assessing his options, he realized he had another goal in mind. His brief experience in the restaurant business had taken hold of him and he now dreamed of someday owning a place of his own. Jr. Miller had no idea that a simple act of kindness would have such an immense impact on his future.

Scott Robey

Chapter Three

"By god, you better learn how to fry fish."

It's possible Jr. Miller might have found his way to Colfax even if Earl Blickenstaff hadn't fractured his arm in an automobile accident. Jr. had made the decision to leave the military and return to Frankfort and upon his return, Dutch Kreisher, manager of the Frankfort Elks Club, offered Jr. his old job as a cook. Though the Elks Club was required to hire him back after his return from the service, Kreisher also increased the young cook's weekly salary to $50, double his salary at the time he entered the Army. He was only 27 years old but Jr.'s dream had intensified of someday owning his own restaurant; it was a dream several of the Elks members had become aware of as well. A number of the members had reverted back to referring to James Miller as Jr.—a name he didn't care for, but he was in no position to register a protest to the members of the club that was providing a very good weekly paycheck.

A few months after he returned to the Elk's Club, an automobile accident intervened in Jr. Miller's future. Earl Blickenstaff was an officer of the Clinton County Bank in Frankfort and a frequent patron of the Elk's club restaurant. He had suffered a broken arm in a car crash and found it difficult to eat while his arm was mending in a cast. Jr. told the banker to order anything he wanted and Jr. would make sure it was prepared in such a way that it could be easily consumed. When Blickenstaff ordered a steak, Jr. would broil the meat and cut it up so the banker wouldn't have to struggle with a knife and fork. Blickenstaff was one of the Elk's Club members who was aware of Jr.'s intentions to someday own his own restaurant. Knowing the Elk's Club cook was a talented young man and, because of the courtesy he had extended to him, Earl Blickenstaff began to keep an eye out for opportunities.

In early June of 1946, Blickenstaff approached Jr. with a business proposition. He had identified a small restaurant he thought could be purchased for a reasonable price. Jr.'s immediate response was that he was in no position to acquire the money needed to buy a business, regardless of how reasonable the price might be; he was still making payments on the furniture he and Mary Ellen had purchased. Blickenstaff told Jr. that money would be no problem. He would put up two-thirds of the purchase price if Jr. would provide the remaining third and be in charge of managing the day-to-day operation of the business. When Jr. told Blickenstaff that the one third wasn't a possibility, he learned that Blickenstaff was prepared to provide a bank loan for it; all Jr. had to do was run the restaurant for the partnership. Blickenstaff warned Jr. that the prospective business probably wasn't exactly what the young entrepreneur had in mind. According to Jr., "He told me it was primarily a beer hall. A real "Saturday night" joint."

The business, Brooks' Restaurant in Colfax, relied on three sources of revenue; cold beer at fifteen cents a bottle, sandwiches, and punch boards. While the beer and sandwiches generated a modest profit, the real income came from the gambling boards. Blickenstaff's only caveat was that Jr. manage the business and allow him, Blickenstaff, to remain a silent partner. Given his position with the bank, he felt public opinion might not be favorable toward a banker who was part owner of a tavern—particularly a tavern like the one they wanted to purchase. He urged Jr. to travel out to Colfax with him to take a look at the place.

The two men went to Colfax the following week to inspect the business and visit with the owner, James A. Brooks. Once on the premises, the two men sat at the bar and inspected the business, never leaving the bar stools where they were seated. According to Jr. Miller, "The place needed cleaned up in the worst way. What I did know was that I'd seen Jim Brooks come to Frankfort and throw dollar after dollar into the Elks Club slot machines. I figured if he could do that, I could take a chance of coming to Colfax and trying to make a go of the place myself." The two men decided they would begin negotiations with Brooks to purchase the business.

Earl Blickenstaff saw the business as a source of discretionary income, especially if he could convince the enterprising young cook from the Elk's Club to manage it. Jr. Miller saw Brooks' Restaurant as the possible first step toward realizing his dream of owning his own business. The three men negotiated a selling price of $10,000. Blickenstaff and Jr. Miller returned to Frankfort and drove straight to the Clinton County Bank. Entering through the front door—Jr. was impressed he was in the company of a man who had keys to the front door of the bank—Blickenstaff led his young, soon-to-be partner through the darkened interior and into his office. He flipped on the desk lamp and pulled a blank loan application from a drawer. He slid the document across the desktop to Jr. and told him to sign the bottom line. When Jr. asked what other information was needed for the application, he was told the only thing the bank needed was his signature. After signing the loan paper, Jr. Miller was now one-third owner, having borrowed his one-third share in the business, in what was to become Miller's Restaurant. A glitch arose one week prior to closing the deal when James Brooks' wife, Pauline, vetoed the sale of the business. Upon hearing of Pauline Brooks' reticence, Blickenstaff and Jr. Miller traveled back to Colfax one weekday evening to talk to the reluctant seller. After a two-hour conversation, Pauline Brooks relented and agreed to sell the restaurant to the partners for the agreed price of $10,000.

L to R: Earl Blickenstaff, Jim Pogue, James L. Miller and James A. Brooks.

Jim Brooks had actually operated the business he was about to sell on two occasions. He had first leased the property in January 1927 from Bert Johns for $25 a month. However, after only eight months, he inexplicably canceled the lease; a W.C. Barnes assumed the remainder of the two-year lease. Shortly after the repeal of the 18th amendment, Brooks bought the former Bert Johns building and the adjacent building from John and Lloyd Waugh in October 1933. After their purchase of the property from Bert Johns, the Waughs had operated the business as a restaurant and Minnie Thurman was managing it at the times of Brooks' purchase. The adjacent building had been purchased from the Colfax Bank after it was taken over from Bert Goff. Brooks reopened the Goff property as a poolroom. Fifteen months after the sale of his Colfax business to the Miller-Blickenstaff partnership, James Brooks purchased the 400 Club in Frankfort from Cecil E. Butler. James and Pauline Brooks divorced in 1953 with Pauline Brooks receiving the 400 Club in the settlement; the name of the business was immediately changed to Polly's 400 Club. Jim Brooks later moved to Indianapolis, where he died at the age of 68 in 1962. His obituary that appeared in the *Frankfort Morning Times*, while stating that two children had survived, made no mention of ever being married to Pauline Brooks.

After closing the deal and then getting through the awkward moment of having his wife witness an attempted murder only 48 hours before taking possession of the business, Jr. Miller walked down the stairs from his apartment, flipped on the lights and began the rest of his life. The first day of Miller's generated $79.39 in sales. The first week's sales totaled $650.44 but, after subtracting food and liquor costs, miscellaneous expenses, and the $100 in cash needed to start the cash drawer, the business showed a net loss for the week of $302.85. By the third week of November, the first month of Miller's ownership, the business generated a net profit of $306.78, of which $102.26 belonged to Jr. Miller with the remainder going to Earl Blickenstaff. Jr. Miller was able to make the first payment on the loan he'd received from the Clinton County Bank to buy his business. The unofficial income generated by the punchboards proved to be as lucrative as Earl Blickenstaff had promised, nearly doubling the profits of the restaurant operation.

Rats, cockroaches and the removal of several rowdy customers aside, the first few weeks of the business were uneventful; business was good, even without the exiled patrons. As his partner had told him, the business was centered on huge beer sales and the heavy play of punchboards that were available on the tavern's counter top. Jr. Miller, having a deft business touch, immediately saw where the profits were. One punchboard generated more profit than the sale of ten cases of beer. The profit from the boards could be increased even more if the big payout of $10 was not hit before the board could be removed from play and deposited in the incinerator. It wasn't really deceptive because every board held the chance of the big payout; it was simply a matter of "tilting" the odds in favor of the house.

Miller's Restaurant, spring, 1947. The Keyes pool hall that became Miller's main dining room is to the left.

Jr. began to assess what other changes he could make to his business. His dream was to run a restaurant that served alcohol, not a tavern that served food. As he shared this vision with people, he was advised to install a grill in the bar area; the move would allow him to cook and still keep an eye on what was going on in the main room. The November 1946 installation of the grill led to the addition of steaks to the menu, although the current clientele rarely spent money on steaks that could be used to buy beer. The grill was installed along the back wall behind the counter and upon firing it up and placing the first steak on its surface, Jr. realized there had been one small oversight in the grill's installation—it had no ventilation; the entire room quickly filled with smoke. After several attempts, the bar area cooking space was finally ventilated where patrons did not risk being overcome by smoke. Mary Ellen Miller couldn't understand why the customers minded the smoke; the first night she'd seen the business, the cigarette and cigar smoke had been more dense than any produced by the grill.

Floor space in Miller's was limited. The business was defined by a long bar, referred to as a "counter", which allowed women to sit there and avoid breaking Indiana law which forbid women to sit at a "bar". Fourteen bar stools lined the counter, with a bench sitting over a radiator at the south end of the bar. The barroom had four and a half booths and there was a small dining area behind the bar where patrons could sit at one of four tables. Jr. had begun to clean his business up; the oiled wood floors were thoroughly cleaned and the balance of the restaurant was scrubbed top to bottom—he was off to a good start. In only a few days he was faced with the possibility that his good start was about to come to a premature end.

One day in late November 1946, two men entered through the door of the barroom. They introduced themselves and told Jr. Miller they were with the Indiana Treasury Department. They had come to remove all gambling devices from the premises. The Treasury Department had led a raid on the Frankfort Elks Club (and other venues) the night before. Several fully operating slot machines had been removed from the club during the raid and destroyed. The state was bent on shutting down all illegal gambling, particularly in Clinton County, which had developed a reputation for being one of the most active gambling counties in the state.

Shaken, Jr. admitted he had employed an "occasional" punchboard in his business and turned over three boards from under the counter. After lecturing Jr. on the fines and possible jail time that would be part of the penalty for being discovered using the boards from that point, the two men departed. Jr. walked to the back room of the restaurant and gathered the remaining fifty boards he had stockpiled; the boards had been generating nearly $150 profit every week. He walked out the back door of the restaurant and began slipping his profit into a roaring incinerator fire $15 at a time.

After watching the last punchboard disappear in the flames, he wandered back into the building. Taking a seat at one of the tables in the small dining area, he pondered what would happen to his fledgling business now that a major profit center had been lost. His dilemma was made more complicated by the news he received from Mary Ellen just three weeks after the arrival of the Treasury men; she was pregnant.

After going upstairs to the apartment to inform Mary Ellen what had transpired in the past hour, Jr. decided to call a man he'd relied on for guidance over the past six years—Ralph Ashley. The Ashleys came to Colfax on the Sunday following the visit from the state treasury and the four sat in the barroom to discuss what might be the next step in attempting to save Miller's from closing less than six months from the day it had opened.

The sale of 35-cent sandwiches and the occasional steak could not be depended on to generate enough extra revenue to replace the state-inflicted losses. The only way to increase beer sales would require allowing the expelled rowdies back into the business, which was considered an unpleasant option. The consensus was that Miller's needed to explore expanding its food service. Jr. had felt an expansion would eventually happen, but had not seen it as a near-term plan. The next question was what should be included on the new menu? The four decided they would experiment with a number of items and then survey customers to see what they liked best. Beginning the following week, a nightly "special" was offered, ranging from fried chicken, to spaghetti, to Irene Ashley's oriental cooking.

Ralph Ashley pointed out how Jr. had enjoyed the catfish served at a place called Sam's in Pittsburg, Indiana. The Ashleys had taken their daughter and son-in-law up to the small diner north of Delphi whenever they had extra gas stamps. His father-in-law was right; Jr. did enjoy the catfish at Sam's. There was one problem—he had no idea how to prepare and cook catfish. When he told his father-in-law about this deficiency, Ralph Ashley offered little solace. He looked his son-in-law in the eye and simply said, "By God, you better learn how to fry fish, or you're going to be shutting this place down pretty soon."

The specials, including catfish, were offered for three weeks. Customers were surveyed during the three-week period to see which of the specials they preferred; the results pointed toward permanently adding catfish to the menu. Just to be sure that catfish was going to become their feature menu item Miller's continued to offer Tuesday night specials.

Jr. Miller's initial experiments with learning how to fry catfish proved to be precarious. His early efforts at frying fish utilized an Army ration pan filled halfway with hot grease, primarily lard. The pan, eighteen inches by twelve inches and only six inches deep, could accommodate less than two pounds of fish at a time and, when the pan was removed from the coal-fired stove, grease invariably splashed onto the stovetop and a fire would erupt. The steady eruption of flames caused some level of concern, even among the most beer-fortified customers in the barroom. Jr. Miller remembers, "We went through quite a few fire extinguishers in those early days."

Jr. knew that if they were to be a standard part of his new menu, he had to find a better way to prepare catfish. He remembered his days at Fort Patrick Henry and the sixty-pound fryers he'd used to prepare 15,000 meals a day for the troops and set off to find a similar fryer for his business. He found a fryer after contacting several restaurant supply companies in

Indianapolis. Cleo Wright installed the large deep fryer next to the barroom grill, replete with adequate ventilation. Evening patrons found they could concentrate on their conversations without having to keep one eye to the back bar to see if they should dash to the door to avoid being incinerated in a fire that might engulf the premises.

By early January 1947 Miller's Restaurant had dropped the evening special experiment and established a menu that included one additional choice besides sandwiches and steaks—fried catfish had been the people's choice as the new menu option. Had the crowds preferred Irene Ashley's oriental cooking, it can only be speculated that the business might have become known as Miller's Chinese Buffet and would probably not have established its nationwide reputation. In 1947, a catfish dinner at Miller's cost $1.25.

Mary Ellen Miller rose each morning at 5:00 a.m. and along with former Brooks' employee, Betty Ann Ferguson, would begin prepping for the breakfast crowd. The Millers had considered dropping breakfast, but with the uncertainty created by the loss of the punchboard income felt they had to continue opening at 6:00 a.m. The restaurant continued to serve lunch with Iva Jackson preparing roast pork sandwiches, breaded tenderloins that emerged from the addition of a small deep fryer, and the restaurant's most popular lunchtime item, brain sandwiches. After Jackson's retirement, Dorothy Haag continued to prepare the best plate lunches in Colfax.

Being four months pregnant, Mary Ellen usually had to deal with the resulting morning sickness and then proceed with breakfast. Beer was served from 8:00 a.m. to closing and it was common to serve bacon, eggs, and Budweiser®. After the purchase the Millers retained the entire Brooks staff including Ferguson, Jackson, Stella Bowen, Raleigh Waggoner, Don Ferguson and night bartender, Bob Saunders. The weekly payroll, including the Miller's $50, totaled $159.00 for the first few months. The expanded food service, including breakfast and lunch, and the newly created night time menu began to generate enough cash flow that the young couple felt they weren't in imminent danger of losing their fledgling business. However, the additional food service ensured the couple would continue working 18-hour days, six days a week.

The loss of the punchboards had created another problem. Jr. Miller had left his $50 a week job at the Elk's Club and began paying himself, and Mary Ellen, $25 a week each. It became obvious after only two months without the gambling income that the weekly salary was not keeping up; the Miller's income had not increased, but their obligations had. Jr. now had to concern himself with the scheduled installments at the Clinton County Bank and he approached his partner to explain his financial situation. Earl Blickenstaff advised Jr. to give himself a raise. When questioned how much the raise should be, his partner said it should probably be at least $20 a week. Jr. returned to Colfax elated with the forty percent increase in his weekly income. Upon returning he assured his wife that they could now hold their own financially. Mary Ellen Miller remembers why she welcomed the raise, "Here we were making $50 a week between us and he (Jr.) had been loaning money to a half a dozen customers. Can you believe that?" Jr. was being repaid, on occasion, but often times he wasn't. Mary Ellen soon put a stop to the customer loans; the impending arrival of a baby necessitated the Millers save any extra income rather than serving as a small loan service.

The business was also beginning to take on a new personality. As part of his plan to attract a dinner crowd (and to place less emphasis on the bar), the partition separating the barroom from the small dining area was repositioned in 1949 to provide more table space. The Millers had installed air conditioning for the restaurant the previous summer. The fact that the small dining area existed at all was due to Jim Brooks' attempt to create an area that was segregated from the rowdies in his barroom. Unlike Jr. Miller, Brooks had not been willing to make the drastic decision to expel his unruly customers. Instead, he made an investment in decorating the vacant area immediately behind the barroom in knotty pine and furnished with tables made by J. C. Jordan's Indiana Hickory Furniture Company. He created the new area hoping to attract a more civilized crowd of both men and ladies. A news article in the March 14, 1935 edition of the *Clinton County Review* reported that Brooks, who the paper called, "that hustling and enterprising restaurant proprietor of Colfax", had added a side entrance to the new room, "that will be more private for patrons not wanting to be bothered by the loafers from the front part of the restaurant." The same edition carried a large display advertisement announcing the opening of the new room that had its own identity, creating a "business within a business" that Jim Brooks hoped would help him expand his clientele. The new space provided only four tables and was called the Hickory Inn; the ad announced in large letters, "Ladies Invited!"

By 1949, Clinton County had returned to its status of being a gambling center in the state. Slot machines had returned to the clubs and punchboards could be found in nearly every tavern in the county except Miller's. Though the punchboards had provided a handsome incremental income in the early days of the restaurant, Jr. Miller realized he had begun to build his business the way he'd always dreamed; he saw no reason to jeopardize it by bringing the gambling boards back.

The repositioned dividing wall allowed for the addition of four tables in the dining area at the expense of seven bar stools. Ralph Ashley continued his energetic support of his son-in-law's business venture by building the new tables for the expanded dining area; the barroom counter now had only seven stools. The newly created space accommodated seating for 36 diners,

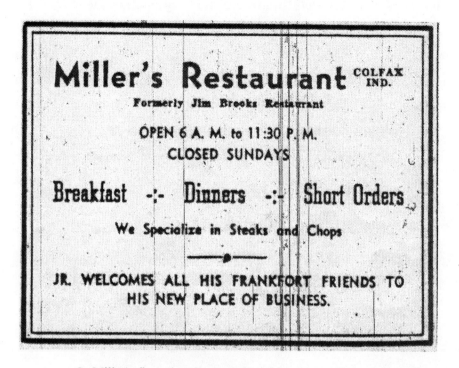

Jr. Miller's first advertisement. *Frankfort Morning Times*,
November 24, 1946.

bringing the seating total for the restaurant to 54. Jr. placed a small ad in the *Frankfort Morning Times* inviting his Frankfort friends out to Colfax for the fried catfish and choice steaks being served at his restaurant. The Frankfort crowd began to show up and created one last identity crisis for Jr. Miller. When he and Mary Ellen moved to Colfax they decided he would return to his alias of Jerry Miller. However, when the Elk's Club bunch began to frequent the restaurant, they would greet Jerry as Jr. The locals immediately jumped on the name and from that point Jr. became the moniker of choice— whether he wanted it or not.

The remaining local crowd was shaping the business' personality. Jr. had made the decision to expel the riffraff, but he made sure he retained a number of the "characters" who were steady customers. These loyal (and relatively well-behaved) patrons formed the cornerstone of Miller's success. According to Jr. Miller, "These people were why we didn't mind the long hours. We had started to have fun with the place, regardless of the long hours."

Mary Ellen Miller was having fun, but she was also pregnant. On January 20, 1948 she gave birth to a son. Given his grandmother Ashley's maiden name and, in tribute to his late uncle, Meikel Frank Miller, the future co-owner of Miller's Restaurant, had arrived.

Colfax, Indiana. 1921

Chapter Four

Nearer my God to thee—a little too near.

The plat for the town of Colfax, then called Midway, was filed in December 1848 and recorded on January 5, 1849. The plat included 69 lots and all streets and alleys were aligned with the Lafayette and Indianapolis Railroad. Railroads played an important role in Midway's early development. The I.C. & L. Railroad commenced in 1848 as the plat of the town was laid out, being completed in 1852. It was later known as the Big Four and then became part of the New York Central System. In 1869, another railroad was started as the L.C. & S.W., giving Colfax and Perry Township the only railroad in Clinton County for over 15 years. The county seat of Frankfort needed a rail outlet and the new L.C. & S.W. line was extended in 1870. The line later came to be known as the Pennsylvania Line and eventually led to Colfax being relegated to "just another little town" by the middle of the twentieth century.

In 1853 when an attempt was made to obtain a post office for the town, it was discovered there was another town of Midway in Spencer County, Indiana. The post office was eventually granted, but under the name of Colfax. The name was chosen in honor of South Bend, Indiana resident Schuyler Colfax, who had recently been elected to the U.S. Congress. In 1850 Schuyler Colfax had been a member of the state constitutional convention that drafted Indiana's present constitution. One of the provisions of the constitution was that no blacks be allowed to settle in the state. Schuyler Colfax later emerged as a leader in the fight against banning blacks from settling in Indiana; he was elected Vice President in 1868. There was a period of confusion immediately following the establishment of the post office when the post office operated under the name of Colfax but residents continued to refer to their town as Midway. The town of Midway officially became Colfax in 1857.

The central business district of Colfax migrated five blocks north of where it was originally platted and became centered near the intersection of the railroads. The town expanded west from the depot and four blocks of business buildings had sprung up by the early 1900s; three blocks along the main street and another block of businesses extended north on Oakland Street. Railroad Street extended due west from the depot and served as Colfax's main street (its name was changed to Main Street in the 1990s). Railroad Street continued to the western edge of Colfax where the Colfax Tile and Drain Company opened in 1900. The company operated until 1923 and was later converted into a furniture factory by L.C. Jordan in 1928. Jordan's first business venture in Colfax had been the construction of the Colfax Grain Elevator. He sold the business to Lake and Reagan in 1927. Owner Lawrence Lake created some notoriety for Colfax, as he became known as one of the shrewdest grain merchants in the Midwest.

With two intersecting railroads at its center, Colfax attracted more than its share of railroad work gangs, transients and shifty ne'er'-do-well's. In the late nineteenth and early twentieth centuries, Colfax had established a reputation of a town so rough that a woman could not consider herself safe on its streets after dark. Booze played a role in the social fabric of Colfax from its earliest days, beginning with a saloon at the corner of Railroad and Clark Streets. Its proprietor, Jerry Sheehan, had migrated to Colfax in 1845 after arriving from his native Ireland. Newspaper articles during its early years chronicled weekly brawls at Sheehan's tavern and around the town's largest hotel near the intersection of the two railroads. One of the most violent incidents occurred near the depot in 1904 between locals and a group of Italian laborers working for the Vandalia Railroad. The brawl sent three local residents and bartender Wid Lane to doctors for emergency surgery to sew up a variety of knife wounds; a number of stray teeth were recovered from the station platform the morning after the clash. Clinton County Prosecutor, George V. Moss, later filed rioting charges against several locals for inciting the brawl by shouting ethnic slurs at the Italians.

The northwest corner of Railroad and Oakland Streets was a busy center of trade from the 1850s on. In 1878 the three storefronts that would all eventually become part of Miller's housed a drug store, J.H. Girt's general store and, a grocery. The corner drug store was purchased in 1902 by George Pendry and became home to his variety store. The Pendrys sold the upper floor to Francis M. Goldsberry in 1904. It's believed that Goldsberry, a prominent local attorney and Civil War veteran, converted the upper floor into a combination hotel and boarding house—or at least it was thought to be a hotel. Given Colfax's licentious reputation, some are of the opinion that the upper floor of the building that eventually became Miller's, including the Miller's home for over four years, might have provided more than just a place for travelers to rest. Since Colfax's other hotel was known to be frequented by a number of ladies who were providing valued service to both the local male population and the railroad work gangs that traveled through the area, it can only be assumed that Goldsberry's hotel might have been utilized accordingly whether he was aware of the activity or not. Bert Johns purchased the entire building in January 1913. Francis Goldsberry was quick to sell to Johns after hearing of Johns' plans to serve beer in his restaurant on the ground floor; Goldsberry died a month after selling the property to Johns. Johns converted the Pendry variety store into a restaurant and continued to operate the hotel on the second floor.

Slightly more than a year had passed and Jr. Miller was building his restaurant business, but he could not escape the fact he also owned and operated Colfax's only tavern. There were some in Colfax who felt that one tavern was one too many; Colfax businessman Earl Anderson led the anti-Miller's group. His furniture business was just one block north of Miller's in a building that had housed the White Restaurant that had been operated by Bert Johns prior to his purchase of the Pendry /Goldsberry property. The Millers discovered in December 1947 just how strong Anderson's opposition to their business actually was. Ralph Ashley had suggested it would be a noble gesture to have a Christmas party for local children. He assumed it could be held in the dining area of the restaurant. The space was separated from the barroom by a walled partition and posed no violation of Indiana liquor laws. The town was excited about the idea and the *Clinton County Review* ran a front-page article announcing Santa's arrival on December 20th and that Santa's headquarters would be at what the *Review* called, Miller's Cafe. Children were to stop by the restaurant to drop off their Christmas list and receive a bag of treats. The newspaper stressed that if a child was sick and unable to attend, that the child should send a letter telling Santa what they wanted for Christmas. The letter was to be addressed to Santa Claus, C/O Miller's Cafe, Colfax. Two days before the party was to be held, Jr. Miller learned that Anderson had arranged for people to be stationed in the post office across the street from the restaurant to gather evidence that the Millers had allowed children in the bar. He had also alerted, as he was thought to have done several times after, the state excise police of the possible violation.

After learning of Anderson's plans, Ralph Ashley decided the party would go on as scheduled—with one small change. He donned a Santa Claus suit and set the children's party up on the sidewalk that ran adjacent to the restaurant, a sidewalk that was in plain view of the sentinels stationed in the Colfax Post Office. Candy, fruit, and a small gift were passed out to every child who attended and one of several attempts by Earl Anderson to close down Miller's was thwarted. To avoid further conflict, the children's Christmas party was moved to Cessna's Store the following December.

Despite the small contingency of resistance to Miller's, weekend business was starting to grow. People were hearing that Miller's was worth the trip to Colfax for dinner, as long as you wanted fried catfish or steak. With the installation of the large fryer, Jr. Miller was preparing as much as sixty pounds of fish on a weekend night. Word had also begun to spread out in the surrounding area about Miller's and within a few months lines of people waiting for a table were beginning to be seen every weekend night.

The growing out-of-town crowds didn't seem to mind the assembly of locals who continued to frequent Miller's; it was still Colfax's only drinking establishment and Jr. had come to an understanding with his local patrons—you're always welcome, just behave yourself. Someone with Jr.'s physical presence and strength was clearly a man who could back up his words with action if anyone chose to step outside the boundaries of the house rules.

Earl Anderson aside, Jr. and Mary Ellen Miller ingratiated themselves to most of the residents of Colfax during the first three years of their new venture; in many cases, good customers often became good friends. These friendships often led to some good-natured kidding with Clem Jenkins and George Lane being the masters of the good-natured prank. Miller's had become a morning gathering place, not only for breakfast, but for just killing a morning drinking coffee. In October 1954, Jr. determined he needed to raise the price of coffee from five to ten cents a cup. Two days after the menu change he arrived at the restaurant to discover a two-man picket line

L to R: George Lane and Clem Jenkins protest Miller's
coffee price increase.

manned by Jenkins and Lane. The two men carried signs protesting the
price increase of coffee to be "unfair to loafers". After a short negotiation
session with the two protesters, Jr. Miller offered free coffee that morning
which convinced the men to drop their signs and return to the restaurant.
Other local regulars, including Earnest "Monk" McKinsey, Clem Royer,
Kizer Craven, Archie Boots and John Raymond "Buck" Lenehan, one of
Colfax's most notorious citizens and a man who would become one of the
Miller's good friends, all provided a lifetime of memories for the Millers.

Other customers like Kip Parr, a Lebanon insurance man, often gave Jr.
Miller a good-natured ribbing. Parr had accused Jr. of not always providing
a full pound of catfish as advertised. One night when Parr was sitting in a
booth in the bar, he decided to prove that Jr. Miller was shorting him on his
fish order. After being served, he picked up his platter of fish and slid from
the booth. After walking to the counter he produced a small set of scales.

As a small crowd gathered to observe the official weigh-in, Parr removed the fish from the platter and stacked them on the scales' platform. When the needle slid across and registered one pound, two ounces the accusation was put to rest.

James L. "Jr." Miller, 1954

Entering 1952, demand for Miller's 54 seats was creating long lines and even longer waits. Jr. Miller had not imagined that people would be willing to wait for a meal in what was now becoming known as his catfish restaurant and he was becoming uneasy with the inconvenience of the wait. Ralph Ashley attempted to ease the customers' wait by performing magic tricks for the people standing around the walls of the restaurant's interior or outside along the sidewalk. A summertime wait was not a problem; many of the diners would either bring their own beer or purchase six packs across Railroad Street at Ivo "Doc" Davis' liquor store. They would sit in their cars until they heard their number blast out from the crackling loud speaker above the side entry door. However, when winter arrived in Indiana, those seeking a table after the interior of the restaurant became stacked with waiting customers were relegated to sitting in their cars with heaters blasting and a window cracked just enough to hear their number called out. With Jr. Miller's inherent dedication to his customers, he felt he had to do something about creating a more comfortable wait.

Fiscal 1950-51 had seen the Miller's business double from its first year and they used their share of the year's profits to buy their first home two blocks north of the restaurant. The small upstairs apartment had become too cramped for the couple and their young son. The Millers paid $5,000 for a house they purchased from Eugene Timmons that has remained their home since. However, even with the purchase of their home and still paying on a portion of the $500 loan for their first automobile, a well-used 1941 Ford purchased in late 1947, Jr. Miller realized another investment had to be made to accommodate the growing crowds of customers.

In October 1952, he approached Harry and Flossie Keyes, owners of the building adjacent to Miller's, to ask them to consider selling their property. He felt that a door could be cut through the wall, allowing for the Keyes' building to be converted into additional table space and an indoor waiting area. Harry Keyes was operating the same pool hall in the space he had purchased from Jim Brooks when Brooks made the decision to sell his restaurant to the Millers; Brooks' wife Pauline and Flossie Keyes were sisters. Keyes owned a custom-baling and trucking business, which he continued to operate after the purchase of Brooks' pool hall. Prior to the Keyes' pool hall, the space had housed a bowling alley, and prior to that, the Colfax Bakery, owned and operated by Bert Goff. Goff had owned the Keyes' property and the adjacent building to the west. However, records show the Colfax Bank took possession of both properties from Goff in October 1934, an apparent victim of the economic conditions of the Depression. The Waughs purchased the Goff property from the Colfax Bank the same time they purchased the hotel and restaurant from Bert Johns.

After some negotiation, the Keyes agreed to sell their property to Jr. Miller for $4,000. Earl Blickenstaff supported the expansion idea. Jr. Miller recalls, "I told Blick before we began the partnership that if he couldn't trust me completely to do the best possible job at running the place and making both of us money, he shouldn't hook up with me. He never questioned a decision I made; he was the perfect partner. It didn't hurt that we made money from the first year on." The only conflict that arose between the partners was early on when it was discovered the restaurant property had been deeded to only Blickenstaff and his wife. The situation was quickly rectified and the partnership went smoothly for several more years.

After the deal was closed, the Millers decided to remodel the entire business. While the entryway from the original dining room into the newly acquired space was being cut, Walter Harrison, Sr. was replacing the old wooden floors and laying new linoleum and Cleo Wright was hired to rewire both sides of the business. The remodeling of the restaurant reflected Jr. Miller's efficient approach to the restaurant. The new decor was anything but flashy—gray linoleum lined the floor and counter and tabletops were covered with Formica®. The "whorehouse red" flocked wallpaper was not applied to the walls of the small dining room behind the bar until 1964; the walls of the new main dining room were covered with a conservative wallpaper.

The remodeling was nearly complete and, combined with the purchase price of the property and cost of improvements, the Miller's had spent nearly $12,000, exhausting all of their cash reserve and borrowing the remainder. Though the business was growing and earning a profit, the new cash outlay was significant; business was going to have to continue to grow to take care of the added debt. Jr. had made tough decisions before and he was certain this new commitment would pay off. He had no idea the State of Indiana was about to intervene again.

The expansion was completed in 1953, but wasn't to open up until early 1954; the Millers needed to accumulate extra cash to add chairs to the new room. As he had done with the first expansion, Ralph Ashley built all the tables for the expanded dining area. The last detail was for Jr. to make sure his cooking capacity would keep pace with the added dining area. After the room was furnished and Jr. was comfortable that he could keep up with increased demand, the new Miller's was ready to open. Two days before they were to open "the new room", as it would be called until early 1971 when another expansion took place, the door to the bar opened and a man, dressed in a dark suit, entered the barroom. He introduced himself to Jr., identifying himself as being from the state Alcoholic Beverage Commission. The commission had learned the Millers had begun an expansion to the west of the existing business. Jr. told the officer that the expansion had not only begun but, for the most part, had been completed—was there a problem?

Railroad Street bound Miller's on the south and intersected with Meridian Street at the far corner heading west. The excise officer informed Jr. that his expansion would put him too close to the Wesleyan Church, which had organized in 1947 and occupied what was once the Stillwell Post #375 of the Grand Army of the Republic building at the northeast corner of Meridian and Railroad Streets. The post had been disbanded in 1913 and the building was sold to the Relief Corps of Colfax that was headed by Sadie Goldsberry, third wife of Francis M. Goldsberry. The building was purchased by Raleigh Higer in July 1936 but was now owned by the members of the newly created Wesleyan Church. The man who was once employed by Miller's to keep the peace inside the barroom had also played a role in Miller's future with the sale of his property to the church.

The state law clearly spelled out that no establishment selling alcohol could be built within 200 feet of a church. The man from the ABC had been told that the expanded restaurant would be too close to the nearby church. Jr. walked outside with the officer and, stretching a tape measure from the western-most wall of the new dining room measured out 100 feet; he then moved farther down toward the church. Coming to a stop, Jr. saw he was clearly standing across the edge of the church property and, even holding the tape loosely, it showed 97 feet. 197 feet—he was 36 inches away from losing $12,000, and possibly his entire business. He and the excise officer walked back to the restaurant. After entering the building, Jr. took the enforcement officer on a tour of the newly remodeled business, explaining in detail the investment of each improvement and that each improvement had already been paid for. The excise man offered a glimmer of hope. He told Jr. that an excise board meeting was being held that evening in

Indianapolis. Since the issue centered on only a few inches, he would propose to the board that an exception be made and that the Millers be allowed to utilize the new expansion; he would call Jr. the next morning to inform him of the board's decision. Jr. rose early the next morning after lying awake the entire night. He walked to the restaurant and spent most of the morning staring at the telephone in the barroom.

The phone rang shortly before noon; the excise officer gave the go-ahead to open the expansion. The Millers had come within 36 inches of losing all the money they had accumulated and possibly their business. Even if money had not been an issue, Jr. knew there would only be a small number of people willing to sit out in freezing temperatures for fried catfish. As expected, church members filed a protest after learning of the special exemption by the ABC; the subsequent hearing allowed the ruling to stand. Without the additional room, Jr. knew his business could never grow. The Millers began to expand as cash flow allowed. What had been set up as a waiting room in the back of the new dining room was decorated and utilized as a dining area in 1962. Its coziness prompted many customers to wait extra time for a vacant table in the "back room" that was the domain of waitress Barbara Kauffman during her many years at Miller's.

Despite the expanded seating capacity for the weekend dinner crowds, the restaurant continued to open for breakfast and serve plate lunches at noon until the early '60s. The business was making money and the Millers wanted to show their gratitude to the community for supporting them; Thanksgiving, 1957 presented them with the opportunity. Invitations were placed in the post office box of every resident of Colfax and an ad was placed in the *Clinton County Review* inviting people to dinner the day before Thanksgiving; there would be a charge of sixty-five cents for the dinner.

Completed remodeling, 1954.

The menu included tomato juice cocktail, relish dish, cranberry sauce, roast turkey and oyster dressing, giblet gravy, mashed potatoes, green beans, apple salad, pumpkin pie with whipped cream, hot rolls, coffee, candy, apples and oranges; complimentary cigars and cigarettes were placed throughout the restaurant. Earl Anderson, who had held a customer appreciation dinner for several years prior to the Miller's event, was quick to point out that the Millers were charging for their meal. Unlike the Miller's full holiday menu, Anderson's free dinner consisted of boiled beans and sandwiches prepared by the women of the Christian Church. Anderson's few pennies worth of free beans compared to the nominal charge for the sumptuous Miller's appreciation meal didn't deter people from attending their event. Over four hundred dinners were served at the Thanksgiving Eve dinner; to the Miller's recollection, Earl Anderson was not among the four hundred. The special dinner was also served on Christmas Eve day and drew an even larger crowd than the Thanksgiving feast. The holiday events were staged through the remainder of the decade.

Earl Anderson owned and operated a business in Colfax beginning in 1924 when he and Rado Shirley bought Leonard Stall's grocery store. The partnership was set up much like the Blickenstaff/Miller arrangement. Shirley purchased the business and inventory with Anderson managing the business. The agreement called for each partner to receive $7 per week and groceries, with Anderson paying for his share of the partnership from his cut of the profits. He managed to complete the purchase of his partnership in only four years. Anderson later purchased the remaining share of the grocery business and about 1930 became the third member of an Indianapolis-based buying group that operated under the Regal® brand name. He later acquired Regal stores in Clarks Hill and Thorntown, operating all three stores as the Anderson Regal Store.

Anderson was considered by most to be an enterprising businessman. He had begun to sell Crosely radios as a side business during his partnership with Rado Shirley. In 1936, Anderson, who once worked as a traveling salesman for a furniture company in Tipton, began attending used furniture auctions in Indianapolis, returning to Colfax to resell his purchases in a storefront in the same building as the grocery, a building he had purchased from Harry Coyner for $2,000 in 1935. His furniture business, which would later include several lines of new merchandise, grew to a point where he decided in 1946 to sell all three grocery stores to concentrate on his furniture business, which operated under the Anderson Furniture Mart name for several years. The Regal store in Colfax was purchased by Jack Boots, who operated it in the original location until building a new store in 1953.

Though he would never be considered congenial, Earl Anderson was by any standard a good businessman and active in the community, often serving as committee chairman for such causes as the March of Dimes. Even with his reputation of being somewhat of a crosspatch, he would have no doubt been successful with his business, at least by Colfax standards, without Miller's attracting customers from far outside what would have been his market area. His only flaw was his inflexibility in tolerating anyone who did not share his moral standards, standards that moved him to be a near fanatical enemy of any business in Colfax that served alcohol.

Anderson was a lifetime member of the Colfax Christian Church where he served as Sunday School Superintendent. He had been consistent in his opposition to any tavern in Colfax, criticizing and lobbying for the closure of Brooks' Restaurant before Jr. Miller and Earl Blickenstaff had purchased it. Anderson was actually carrying on the crusade to ban taverns in Colfax that had begun in earnest during the early years of the 20th century. Many of Colfax's tipplers had done their part to provide fodder for those who were fighting the crusade for a constitutional amendment to ban the sale of liquor. In 1906, Francis M. Goldsberry, who at the time owned the property that would eventually become Jr. and Mary Ellen Miller's apartment home, had been successful in gaining a blanket remonstrance in all of Perry Township that created a two year ban on the new opening of any, what an article in the *Thorntown Enterprise* called, "jag factories". The article went on to say, "It is a fact that the saloon business in Colfax for the past 25 years has been one prolonged tragedy draped in tears, moans, half-clad children, brutalized mothers and many homes that were but a little better than hovels." The article commended Goldsberry and, "the other pillars of the church" for having the courage to push the successful remonstrance. Goldsberry's zealous opposition to the consumption of alcohol led to his decision to sell his upstairs property to Bert Johns after his purchase of the Pendry variety store and its subsequent conversion to a "jag factory". The 1906 article substantiated that the Millers were being confronted with building a reputable business in the face of 75 years of dubious history.

Anderson's efforts intensified when the Millers took over from Jim Brooks, presumably because it was becoming clear to Anderson that Miller's was beginning to grow in popularity. Anderson pressured Tress McKinsey, at the time Editor of the *Clinton County Review,* to write an editorial condemning Miller's presence in Colfax. McKinsey informed Anderson she would be glad to publish a letter to the editor, but it would have to be signed. Anderson, probably assuming he was in a minority among Colfax residents, declined to write a letter with his signature attached. Though Anderson worked tirelessly to oppose Miller's, the Reverend Ernest Fitch, Minister at the Colfax Christian Church, became good friends with the Miller family. All the churches in Colfax had active memberships and had played an important role in transforming the town into a tamer, family-oriented place to live. However, most church members were not as fervid in their opposition to Miller's as Anderson.

Possibly with the inspiration of F.M. Goldsberry's successful remonstrance as motivation, Anderson attempted to gain support for the closing of Miller's when he began to gather signatures on a petition that was to be sent to the state Alcoholic Beverage Commission accusing the business of being a nuisance and in violation of a number of unspecified commission laws. Loyal Miller's customers who had seen the petition were outraged at Anderson's efforts. They told Jr. that he should build a fence around his business and secede from the incorporated town, suggesting that the newly created town be called Millerville.

The national prohibition of alcohol had been successful in closing all but one tavern in Colfax for good. However, when Anderson attempted to gain support for his petition it appeared that even the most devout church goer didn't seem to mind having one tavern in Colfax, especially the way Jr. Miller appeared to be operating his; he had managed to throw out the derelicts that had caused the most problems after a long night of swilling beer in the former Brooks' tavern. When Anderson acquired only a handful of signatures, he dropped the ABC complaint effort. It was apparent that social attitudes had changed since F.M. Goldsberry's days, especially as townspeople were beginning to see how the Millers were reinventing the old Brooks' Restaurant.

Miller's began evolving into a family restaurant by the early 1950s, but Jr. Miller still had ways of catering to his local barroom clientele. He began a tradition in 1954 of distributing calendars that Hugh Hefner would have been proud to run in his fledgling men's publication. The 1954 edition was particularly noteworthy in that it carried a photograph of a completely nude Marilyn Monroe. Within two years and after she had been discovered by Hollywood film studios, the photograph was never released again without the beautiful Miss Monroe covered with a black negligee that had been airbrushed over the original photograph. Jr. didn't know at the time that he was distributing a photograph that would later become a valuable collector's item.

There are ironies in Earl Anderson's opposition to Miller's. He would have probably been unwilling to accept that Jr. Miller, despite being a tavern owner and having a well-known reputation as a hard drinker, was also a devout believer in God, a belief that led him to resist opening on Sunday. "I promised the Lord, and you don't tempt the Lord, that if he would give me the energy and wisdom to be successful in my business, I would never be open for business on Sunday." In its 49 years of operation, Miller's served customers on Sunday only once.

The Colfax High School basketball team had competed in the Lafayette regional of the state basketball tournament after upsetting Rossville to win the 1957 Frankfort sectional. They defeated Thorntown in the afternoon game of the regional, coming back to win after missing all but one of their first eleven shots. Dick Ham, writing for the Lafayette *Journal and Courier* called the Colfax win, "the gamest comeback in tournament history." The fact the win had come against Colfax's archenemy from Boone County made the win even sweeter. The Colfax Hickories of coach Gene Hendryx, (the school nickname coming from Colfax's own "Home of Handsome Hickory") lost the evening championship to Lafayette Jefferson after holding a ten point lead at one time in the game. Lafayette Jefferson coach, Marion Crawley, was quoted after the game, "I guess Colfax was tougher than the boys and I thought." Colfax teams, while not always long on talent, were known for an inherent toughness that reflected the historical roots of the town. In 1957, they had combined toughness with talent and had given the much taller Broncos all they could handle. It was the Hickories' first (and last) regional appearance and they performed admirably against their big city rival.

People in Colfax wanted to celebrate and asked Jr. Miller to host a dinner honoring the team, which included all-regional team picks, George Newell and Russell Heilman. Heilman, standing at 5' 6' and only a junior, had been described by *Journal and Courier* Sports Editor Gordon Graham as, "erratic, but he is sensational too...the little guy was the "people's choice" in the last part of the Thorntown game and the early part of the Jeff contest." The dinner was hosted at Miller's on Sunday, April 14, 1957 and was attended by 184 people The program included speeches by each player and cheerleader except for senior Ted Newell who was struck with appendicitis during dinner and rushed to the hospital. The banquet was a private affair, making it only a minor violation of Jr. Miller's "never on Sunday" policy.

The second irony of Earl Anderson's opposition lay in the impact Miller's had on Anderson's furniture business. As the lines, and the wait for a table grew longer, Anderson extended the business hours of his furniture store on Wednesday and Saturday nights. Given the proximity of the restaurant to the furniture store, people could come into Anderson's business, browse and still be able to hear their number being broadcast out on the outside loud speaker. As the number of people from cities like Indianapolis increased, they discovered that Anderson carried many of the same lines of furniture that his large city counterparts stocked, only at greatly reduced prices. Anderson's sales volume went up significantly as he shipped more and more furniture to customers outside of Colfax. Anderson was quoted in a 1971 newspaper feature about Colfax that people came there for more reasons than to eat catfish, for example, to buy furniture. He seemed to have conveniently forgotten that a number of his steady customers would have never discovered his business had it not been for Miller's providing the initial draw.

Jr. and Mary Ellen Miller acknowledge that Anderson eventually became civil to them after finally realizing how significant his economic windfall had been due to the Miller's restaurant business. However it might have also been because Anderson came to realize the Millers were operating a legitimate restaurant business and not a tavern. After watching the throng of people enter Miller's, including hundreds of families with small children,

Anderson most likely came to the conclusion that James L. Miller had brought something to Colfax that had been beneficial to the community. He most likely wouldn't have posted sentries in the post office if Miller's had hosted a children's Christmas party in the '70s.

Jr. Miller's reputation as a hard drinker was legendary among Colfax residents, a situation he admits he's not proud of. Yet, anyone who has ever known him would quickly come to his defense and point out that they never observed him incapacitated. Those who dined in the booths that lined the bar room wall might claim they never saw Jr. drink while he was manning the fryers. However, they would observe him sipping from a salad bowl that was kept within arm's reach on a shelf above the fryers. Most thought it was soup, when in reality the bowl was kept full of Lord Calvert® whiskey. Jr. Miller contends, "I finally drank them out of business. When somebody else opened up a distillery in Canada and was supposedly selling the same stuff, I could tell that it wasn't. That's when I switched to scotch. I'm not proud of it, but I was a quart a day scotch drinker." The salad bowl was now filled with J&B®. There were a number of salesmen who called on Miller's who would find themselves sipping mid-morning highballs with its owner. Most would leave to go home to sleep off their sales call, while Jr. would carry on unaffected for the balance of the business day.

As his son reached school age, Jr. was faced with a dilemma. His partnership with Earl Blickenstaff had remained silent; very few people were aware of Blickenstaff's involvement in the business even though official records showed the transfer of the James Brooks property going to Blickenstaff in 1947. In 1953, Blickenstaff had sold a portion of his share to his partner that balanced the partnership from the original 2/3-1/3 to a 50-50 position. Jr.'s concern was for his son. He was unsure if others were aware of the partnership and he had operated Miller's Restaurant with people believing him to be the sole owner. He feared a schoolmate might confront his young son with the truth about his father's operating relationship with Earl Blickenstaff. He was unsure how Mike might respond; he had spent his first six years thinking his father to be the sole owner of the family's business. By this time Mike Miller had begun to understand his father's goal of transforming the original business from its saloon image. Once, when being introduced to the newly appointed minister of the Methodist Church, his Sunday school teacher introduced Mike condescendingly by commenting, "Mike's father owns the local tavern." Mike quickly corrected the woman by pointing out to the minister that his father owned the local restaurant; the minister of the Methodist Church became a frequent customer.

After wrestling with the possibility of disappointing his son, Jr. approached his partner with a proposition: one of the partners had to buy the other's interest in Miller's Restaurant. Earl Blickenstaff quickly responded that he had no desire to run a restaurant and he was certain if he purchased his partner's share of the business he would not be able to find anyone to manage it as capably as Jr. Miller had demonstrated during the eight years of their partnership. Earl Blickenstaff expressed his understanding of his partner's dilemma and that there was only one solution to Jr.s situation—he would sell his 50 percent of the business. Blickenstaff didn't relish giving up his portion of the returns from an astute personal investment or, what he called his "vacation money". The two partners reached a buy-out agreement that would span over a five-year period. The only contract executed in the agreement was a handshake and, for those who knew Earl Blickenstaff, the handshake was as binding as any written contract. Jr. Miller remembers the precise moment, "Blick reached out, shook my hand and said, "It's been a pleasure doing business with you." I asked him if we needed to write up a formal contract. He told me we just had. A handshake. That was the way he worked. He was quite a man." On November 8, 1960 the property was transferred and Miller's Restaurant was in sole possession of the Miller family.

Chapter Five

"I had some peculiar ideas."

By 1953, Jack Boots owned the only grocery store in Colfax. Boots built his new grocery on property where the St. George Catholic Church had once stood; the church was disbanded in 1917 and later dismantled. The land continued to be owned by the Diocese of Lafayette for the next 36 years until it was deeded to Boots by the Most Reverend John G. Bennett, Bishop of the diocese. Boots, and subsequent owners of the grocery store, including Colfax native, Richard Timmons, would make sure they always stocked an ample supply of women's hosiery, especially on weekends when working at Miller's sometimes became a contact sport. It was not uncommon to see a woman, dressed in a bright white uniform, come sprinting into the store, head directly toward the supply of hose, snatch a package from the shelf, throw the money for the purchase on the counter and disappear. Waitresses at Miller's who had neglected to place extra hosiery in their purses before departing for work and, who suffered the unexpected run in their hose, were expected to depart the restaurant regardless of how busy they were to make the one block dash to the grocery store to purchase a replacement pair. Jr. Miller would not tolerate defective hosiery as part of the uniform, even when it happened on the job; it wasn't his only rule for working in his restaurant.

Part of Jr. Miller's dedication to taking care of his customers was manifested in his obsession with cleanliness. "I had some peculiar ideas by today's standards about how I wanted things done, but I just believed it was the only way a place of mine was going to be run. If you couldn't live by my rules—you hit the street." Waitresses were expected to dress in freshly pressed, bright white uniforms. Connie Pritchard, who worked at Miller's for 30 years, was a benefactor of this unrelenting rule. "There was this one waitress who continued to show up with her uniform full of wrinkles. Finally, after several warnings, Jr. told her she was done. I was taken off the salad station and went to waiting tables that night—I did that for nearly 25 years." In later years, Jr. relented and allowed waitresses to wear colored aprons. Shoes were to be polished a bright white before each shift. Jr. would tell his staff, "If your shoes are dirty, what will people think about your underclothes?" He also demanded that nail polish be perfect and strictly forbid the wearing of dangling earrings; customers would often comment to waitresses that the staff looked more like they should be working in a hospital than a restaurant.

His obsession extended to the facility. Every corner of the restaurant had to be cleaned before waitresses could leave; Jr. didn't leave the thorough cleaning to chance. Dee Rhodes tells the story of how the boss would leave dimes in the dark corners of the restaurant and in the restrooms before he would depart for the evening with his signature comment, "Clean her up pretty girls!" The following day he would check his "traps". If the money had disappeared, he was confident the area had been attended to. It was a small investment for the peace of mind brought on by knowing the restaurant had been thoroughly prepared for the next day's customers. Only one bus boy was employed in the earliest years and waitresses were expected to restock all dishes, clean, and cut the butter for the next night. Dairies had not begun selling individual servings of butter and the waitresses had to take a small wire cutter and slice a single stick of butter into individual servings. Each pat would then be slid onto a small waxed paper square. The following day's butter supply had to be prepared before the wait staff left for the evening.

Jr. Miller guarded his waitresses as though they were his own daughters. No customer was allowed to give one of his waitresses any trouble—verbal or physical. He knew his staff and was confident they provided the best service of any restaurant in the area. When a dispute arose, he would appease the disgruntled customer with a complimentary dinner, but he would never apologize for his waitress. Anyone making lewd comments to a waitress was automatically invited to leave the restaurant—either on his own or under Jr.'s guidance. Any man who inappropriately touched a waitress would count himself lucky if he still had full use of his arms after Jr. Miller was done dealing with him. The local man who once called Mary Ellen Miller a "bitch" was not so fortunate. The man departed the restaurant and was chased down to be the recipient of a broken nose and two blackened eyes.

Jr. also kept his business interests in mind when looking out for his staff. It was difficult to find good help, especially as the crowds began to grow. He couldn't afford to lose a waitress once one came along who proved she could operate under the stress of a weekend night. The energy that made his staff of waitresses so effective, often carried over to their personal lives—especially the sex lives of some. Jr. kept an ample supply of condoms under the barroom counter, purchasing them a gross at a time. He recommended to his waitresses that they help themselves to the supply when dating, or planning an encounter with their husband. Some of the waitresses attributed Colfax's slow population growth to Jr. Miller's concern for his staff of waitresses.

While Jr. Miller was perceived by the outside world as a relentless task master, the majority of his employees understood that the "Miller way" was why the business was enjoying its success and why waitresses working at the restaurant were banking incomes that could not be earned anywhere else.

Nancy Dowell, who was employed by Miller's for 23 years, confirms the opportunity to make a good living. She had started at Miller's in the kitchen and later worked as a salad maker for three years. When a waitress position finally came open, she was moved off the salad bar. "I'd been making $75 a week on the salad bar; the first night I worked I took home $75 in tips. I went home and spread the money out on the bed and my husband couldn't believe it was for one night's work—and it wasn't even a weekend night."

But there was more to working at Miller's than the potential income. Connie Pritchard sums up her experience of being part of the Miller's staff, "When you're working for someone who treated you like family, you just developed an attitude that you'll do anything for them. Jr. and Mary Ellen took care of us—they returned loyalty with loyalty. You just didn't want to ever let them down." Suilon Benjamin, a 15-year veteran of Miller's, concurs. "We couldn't stand the thought of leaving them short-handed." Benjamin serves as a striking example of the dedication of so many of the Miller's staff. She severed the ends of two fingers in a lawn mower accident one afternoon before reporting to work. After a trip to a hospital emergency room to have the fingers securely bandaged, she arrived at work on schedule—a story that would unlikely happen in today's restaurant business when so many staff members are absent simply because "they don't feel like coming to work".

Jr. Miller wanted his waitresses to give their full attention to the customers. Waitresses were not allowed to congregate in the middle of the restaurant to avoid ever having their back turned toward the customers. Suilon Benjamin again, "If two or three of us were standing together Jr. would come by and comment, 'If lightening would hit this spot I'd lose my entire staff'; we'd disperse quickly." There are many stories of the dedication to the Miller family.

Suilon Benjamin and Mary Ellen Miller, July 1995

Stella Bowen was part of the original deal. She'd worked at Brooks' Restaurant as a dishwasher for several years prior to the Miller's ownership, earning a weekly salary of $15 at the time of its purchase. She and her husband, John, better known to locals as Nicky Jack, lived less than three blocks from the restaurant. For most it would be considered an advantage living so close to your place of employment. It would have been for Stella, or Stelly as friends called her, as well—the only problem was that Stelly Bowen couldn't walk. An ulcerated vein had left her without the use of one leg and three blocks may well have been three miles; but Stelly needed to work. The Millers offered numerous times to come by her house to pick her up for work, but Stelly Bowen always said she'd get there on her own.

Rather than rely on someone to come after her, she devised her own unique method of transportation; she would use an old Radio Flyer® wagon. Kneeling on her debilitated leg in the wagon, she would use her other leg to push herself the three blocks to the restaurant's kitchen door. After working an eight-hour shift washing dishes she would return home in the wagon. During inclement weather, particularly snow and ice, she had a spiked shoe that would afford her the extra traction needed to get to work. She made the six block round trip to the kitchen door of Miller's for nearly 30 years.

One day in 1966 a farmer's wife came to Miller's looking for a job.

Stella Bowen

Those who knew the rigors of working as a waitress at Miller's would have been reluctant to attempt a seven hour plus shift after spending the earlier part of the day baling hay in the hot July sun, but it's exactly what Velera Cain often did. She and her husband, Paul, had moved from White County, Indiana, to a Montgomery County farm only a few miles from Colfax. She and Paul had begun to frequent Miller's and, in 1966 when Velera applied for a part-time job at the restaurant she was hired full-time. After a short stint working with Jr. in the front of the restaurant, she was moved to a waitress position. "I'd never worked for anyone before and had no idea what to expect," she says. Velera Cain was no stranger to hard work. The Colfax Grain Company employed Cloyse Street, Avis Davis' brother. He often told his sister that there was no man who could unload corn faster than Velera Cain.

The late Paul Cain had his own stories about his wife. During one planting season, while unloading bagged fertilizer into their corn planter, he would pick up a single bag and empty it into the planter—Velera would do likewise. He then picked up two bags, carrying one under each arm to the planter to be unloaded and his wife did the same. Enough was enough; Paul Cain told people he said to his wife, "You're crazy if you think I'm carrying three."

As farm savvy as Velera Cain might be, she is also a strikingly elegant woman. She would come off the tractor, get dressed, and make the fifteen-minute drive to Colfax, usually arriving within a minute of the start of her shift. Her blond hair and brilliant white uniform usually glowed against the deep tan she'd acquired in the corn and hay fields of her family farm—few who came to Miller's would have guessed how she'd spent the majority of her daytime hours.

Cain epitomized the service people came to expect at Miller's. "I had so many good, loyal customers," she says. Other waitresses, without any hint of jealously, relate how many customers would wait an extra half hour for one of Cain's tables. She wasn't the only waitress who people were willing to wait for; nearly every one had a clique of loyal patrons. According to Velera Cain, "All of us were really picky—even about the chairs we had at our tables. We wanted to make sure our customers were comfortable, so we'd put our names on the bottoms of the chairs to make sure when they waxed the floors every Sunday that they put our chairs back at our tables. The first thing we'd do on Tuesday is move our chairs back if they were at the wrong tables."

While one customer once referred to Jr. Miller as a slave driver, drawing the wrath of the waitress who heard the comment, Velera Cain simply saw her boss as a good businessman. "It's the way he wanted things done. It's why people came back and why all of us could make a very good living working for him." For Velera Cain, her 31 years at Miller's provided a very good living; her income from working at Miller's generated the resources to send nine of her twelve children through college.

Mary Ellen Miller is effusive in her praise of those who helped the Millers build a business. "It would have been impossible to do what we did without the people. Loyal—loyal doesn't even come close to describing so many of the people who were part of our family all those years." Stella Bowen, Velera Cain and Suilon Benjamin are only a few of the loyal employees who helped build Miller's reputation. From the beginning, people like Betty Ann Ferguson, June Davis, Avis Davis, Mary Lou Norton (daughter of Loyd Hankins), Mary Margaret Walton, Jeanette Leopard, Ermadine Lawler, Connie Pritchard, Georgie Lanum, Bernice Morrow and a host of other dedicated staff helped define the Miller's "way of doing business."

Velera Cain. 1971

Mary Ellen Miller has a special place in her heart for Bernice Morrow who was a member of the Miller's staff for 27 years; she had worked as a foreman at the Colfax Furniture Company prior to coming to Miller's. "Bernice and I became close, close friends. I know when you're an owner you're not supposed to get close to the help, but that might be why so many places have trouble with their help nowadays, but Bernice and I were close. Since Jr. and I never had time away from the restaurant, Bernice would keep us up on what was going on around town. She and Georgie Lanum knew about every affair that was going on and every juicy tidbit." The tidbits often included details of affairs going on among certain members of Colfax's local churches.

Avis Davis, Morrow's sister and herself a former Miller's waitress, relates the story about her sister that epitomizes the rapid pace of a typical night at the restaurant. "The entry from the old part of the restaurant to the main room was on an incline. One night Bernice was scurrying down through the doorway to the old room, slipped and fell flat on her back. When somebody helped her up and asked if she was all right, she turned to them and said, 'Hell yes I'm all right. You can't afford to get hurt around here—it's too damn busy.' She never missed a step."

Those who proved their mettle in working under the pressure of a busy weekend night at Miller's found they were targets of recruitment by other restaurant owners. Few ever left Miller's voluntarily; it would be a rare opportunity that could duplicate the income potential of Miller's or the support of its owners. One waitress whose husband was transferred to a job in Illinois discovered how far-reaching Miller's reputation for service was. After applying for a waitress position at a local restaurant she was hired immediately after the owner saw her Miller's experience on the application, explaining, "If you can work at Miller's that long, you can work any place in the country."

Miller's waitresses became known for their customer service, gaining favor by fussing over each customer and, often loading up extra large servings of salad and french fries. Jr. Miller, always cognizant of his bottom line, would halfheartedly chide his waitresses for the unusually large servings by telling them, "you're just suppose to feed 'em girls—not fatten 'em up." Yet Jr. was always quick to take care of the rare customer who was less than satisfied with their experience at Miller's. A letter in the Miller's file was sent to a man who had written to Jr. Miller complaining that he felt his waitress had short-changed him by $1; the letter was written six weeks after the customer's visit. The letter from Jr. Miller offered apologies for the oversight and included a dollar bill.

The two women the Millers, father and son, admit played the most significant roles in the business were their wives. Mary Ellen, and later, Mike's wife, Beckie, were part of the business every day; from serving as waitress, to bussing tables, to running the number line, to bookkeeping and other administrative tasks related to the restaurant. Mike Miller says, "If we hadn't been married to them my father and I couldn't have afforded to hire either one of them."

Beginning with Mary Ellen Miller, the success of Miller's is foremost a story of the women who were part of the restaurant's history. However, one man also played a significant role in shaping the personality of the business. Loyd "Hank" Hankins first entered the Miller's life as a customer. Hankins lived in Colfax, but worked for the Kentland Dairy Products Co. in Mulberry where he operated a route in the western part of Clinton County. He would return to Colfax and come into the bar in the late afternoon, often staying late enough to be the last customer to leave at closing.

In the summer of 1948, Jack Boots and other local businessmen brought a carnival to Colfax as part of the town's centennial celebration. Hankins approached Jr. with the offer to help out on centennial weekend, assuming the restaurant crowd would be larger than usual. Jr. told Hank that he didn't think it would be a good idea since Hank would probably drink up the majority of what he would earn.

Loyd "Hank" Hankins, Santa, Jr. and Mary Ellen Miller. 1953

However, Jr. relented and told Hankins that he would pay him a dollar an hour for the two evenings. Hankins rationalized that he would probably go to Thorntown, which now had its own tavern, and drink at a pace of a dollar an hour. He figured he'd be up two dollars an hour if he stayed in

Colfax to work at Miller's. After finally convincing Jr. to hire him full time, Loyd Hankins gave up his milk route in late October 1949 and came to work for the Millers.

"Hank was like an older brother to me," Jr. Miller remembers. The two grew to be close friends and acted like brothers often do; playing hard, arguing, and confiding their most intimate thoughts. Hankins worked as an assistant manager and, on the rare occasions the Millers would take vacations from their business, operated the restaurant as if it was his own— it never missed a beat under his watch. In the several years preceding his death, Loyd Hankins abandoned drinking and became an active member in Colfax's Christian Church. Though he served as a Deacon in the church, Hankins told members that he would continue to work for his friend. Loyd Hankins died on August 25, 1982. According to Jr. Miller, "The day Hank died was one of the saddest of my life."

While many business owners and senior executives of large companies often describe their employees as "one big happy family", it is often quite the opposite; but at Miller's employees were treated like family. In the early days of the business, Jr. Miller would take his entire staff on trips to Chicago—staying overnight in a luxury hotel and attending shows that someone from Colfax was unlikely to ever see. Former Miller's employees who frequented other restaurants with Jr. noted that he was as demanding of others as he was his own staff. He was sometimes disappointed, particularly when it came to customer service.

On one occasion while dining at one of Cincinnati's finest restaurants he was impressed by the meal, but equally unimpressed with the poor service and attitude offered up by the waiter attending the table. After completing the meal and receiving the check, Jr. rose from the table and walked to the maitre d' to make an unusual request; he wanted to meet the restaurant's

Chicago trip, 1953. L to R: Bernice Morrow, Jr. Miller, Dorothy Haag, Ralph Ashley, Mary Ellen Miller, Mary Margaret Walton, Loyd Hankins, Ermadine Lawler, Mary Lou Norton.

head chef. Reluctant at first, the maitre d' relented and led Jr. into the kitchen. Upon meeting the chef, Jr. reached into his pocket, removed his money clip, and peeled off a $50 bill. Handing the money to the chef, Jr. said, "Your food was marvelous, it's a shame the service detracts so badly from it." He turned and walked from the kitchen, leaving the chef with a stunned expression. Jr. paid the exact amount of the meal check and departed as the offending waiter fumed in the center of the dining room.

Employment at Miller's was often a family affair; it was not unusual for a mother to work alongside her son or daughter. There were few teenage boys in Colfax who weren't employed to bus tables at Miller's. Some criticized the Millers for employing high school students in a business that served alcohol. These people were often confronted by Loyd Hankins who would quickly point out the value of the work ethic imparted to their young employees by the Millers and, that if these youngsters weren't employed, they might be using their idle hours to create trouble. At its peak, Miller's employed over fifty people; all, for the most part, were residents of Colfax or nearby communities. In the later years of ownership by the Miller family, the restaurant actually hired grandchildren of the staff that had been employed in the late 1940s.

It became more difficult for the Millers to make the Chicago trips as the staff numbers increased. However, it didn't stop them from holding employee parties that sometimes went on all night. It was not unusual for the staff to close the restaurant on a Friday or Saturday night, clean the premises and then make the short trip up the street to the Miller home, arriving en masse for a night of partying. Jr. Miller explains, "As hard as these people worked for us, my house was always open when they wanted to have some fun." Alyne Hodges, a 24-year employee of Miller's, had adamant praise for being part of the Miller's family. "They were so good to us; they were good to everybody. It didn't matter what your job was, you were treated like you were the most important person on the staff—they made you feel like the place couldn't run without you. That just made you want to work that much harder."

The frequent parties once prompted Loyd Hankins' wife, Lucille to declare that the restaurant, "was nothing but Miller's fun house up there." Loyd Hankins hired his wife a few months later and, after experiencing the excruciatingly hard work of the day-to-day operation, reversed her opinion, declaring, "Anybody who works this hard deserves some fun." The addition of a swimming pool to the Miller's backyard in April 1958 presented another reason to frequent the boss' house. The installation of an in-ground swimming pool was significant enough to earn a front-page feature in the *Clinton County Review* exalting the luxury of having a swimming pool in the Miller's backyard.

A few years later the Millers would again become the talk of Colfax when they purchased the town's first color television; they actually purchased two color televisions. Jr. Miller first purchased a color television for the barroom section of the restaurant, rationalizing to his wife that it would provide a nice diversion for people waiting for tables. It was actually a shallow reason, since in 1959 when the television was purchased, the few shows being broadcast in color were aired on Sunday night, a night when Miller's was closed. The real reason for the purchase of the new television was to provide a larger screen so local patrons could watch professional boxing that was broadcast on Saturday nights. After Mary Ellen Miller dismantled her husband's lame excuse about the television in the bar, Jr. Miller relented and purchased a set for the couple's home. Had the *Clinton County Review* not ceased publication in August 1958 the arrival of Colfax's first color televisions would probably have been a front-page feature story.

Jr. Miller's home was a gathering place for employees, customers and friends. It was not unusual for him to invite customers to his home—with full access to a well-stocked bar—to wait while their table came available. Other friends would often arrive in the early morning hours to initiate impromptu parties that would carry on until dawn. The success of Miller's, while not making the Miller family wealthy, did allow for some luxuries, especially by Colfax standards. Jr. and Mary Ellen Miller became accustomed to a living room full of kids after purchasing the color television. Their swimming pool also was a magnet for large numbers of teenagers during the summers that followed its installation.

Jr. Miller's exacting standards were also manifested in the food he served. He is succinct in revealing the secret to the success of his restaurant: "Clean grease." While most know the success of Miller's was far more complex than keeping the cooking grease clean, it does epitomize his unwavering operational philosophy that led to the business' wide-spread reputation. The consistently light flavor of the fried catfish was a product of a grease cleaning process that was carried out every night after the close of business. Deep fryers were drained and the oil returned back through special filters specifically designed for the restaurant by Commercial Filters in Lebanon, Indiana.

The quality of catfish served at Miller's was always under scrutiny. Miller's first purchased its supply of fresh catfish from a Lafayette distributor when the decision was made to make it a permanent menu selection. With the growing nightly demand, Jr. decided to investigate the possibility of arranging for direct shipments of catfish from Florida, the source of the local distributor's supply. Florida fishermen were contacted to discuss the prospect of shipping Miller's fish directly to Colfax. The railroad that had served as a hub for Colfax and had once transported young men from throughout the county to their assignments during the Civil War would now become a path for fresh catfish pulled from Florida's Lake Okeechobee. Miller's received its first direct shipment of catfish from Florida in 1948. The fish were packed in metal containers and slid into wooden barrels. The space between the steel containers and barrel walls was packed with ice. Miller's would receive two to three shipments of fresh fish each week. After arriving at the Colfax depot, the local stationmaster would load the barrels onto a cart and push them the two blocks to the restaurant.

The fish arrived only semi-dressed; heads had been removed and a quick cut on either side allowed the removal of most of the fish's interior. Upon arrival at the restaurant, the kitchen staff would finish the preparation, removing any remaining intestines and skin. The "butt hole" would be removed, and the fish was scored on each side. Jr. Miller offers no other scientific term for "butt hole" other than, "Most restaurants that served catfish left them in; we just felt like we should cut it out. I don't know what else you would call it—it was just the fish's butt hole."

When the train depot closed in the late 1950s, Miller's supply of fish continued to be sent by rail, but shipments had to be picked up at the depot in Lafayette. Buck Lenehan would make the twenty-mile drive in his livestock truck to pick up the fish. Lenehan was paid $5 for each 100 pound barrel he delivered. By 1959, Miller's was receiving two shipments a week, six barrels on Tuesday and 14 to 16 barrels on Thursday. Three years later, the railroad stopped shipping the fish, making transportation by refrigerated truck necessary. Freight costs had risen and Miller's received a single shipment each Wednesday. The shipment size ranged from 1,500 pounds to as much 3,000 pounds during the busy summer months. However, shipping costs never precluded the Millers from ensuring that their customers never went without catfish. On more than one occasion when it appeared the restaurant's catfish supply might be running short for the weekend crowd, chartered planes were sent to Florida to pick up additional supplies; George Mikelsons piloted one such special trip. Flying a four seat aircraft with all but the pilot's seat removed, he flew to Florida and returned with the small aircraft packed with the maximum allowable cargo of fresh fish. Mikelsons went on to found the Ambassadair travel club and ATA Airlines, which today operates as Amtran, Inc. where he serves as Chairman.

The Stokes Fishery in Florida became an "accumulator" for Miller's, contracting Miller's fish with a number of individual fishermen and then preparing the shipment. When large single shipments became necessary, Jr. traveled to Florida to investigate methods for avoiding freezing portions of each week's shipment and still retain freshness; it was there he discovered the technique of "glazing". Another expansion of the restaurant was completed in 1971, motivated largely by the need for additional cooler space. The new expansion added the type of cooler that allowed Miller's to spray water on the fresh fish and a quick freeze created an icy glaze over the fish, without actually freezing the fish itself. The glazing prevented air from reaching the fish; Jr. Miller compares it to sealing jelly with paraffin.

Jr. Miller had implacable standards for his signature dish; he wanted only channel catfish that he refers to as split-tails. The channel catfish (Ictalurus punctatus) is one of the more genteel among the nearly 2,000 species of cats—some aficionados sometimes refer to the channel catfish as a "prairie trout" or "whiskered walleye". Large quantities of channel catfish began to be pond raised in the Delta region of the United States in the 1960s. The size of the fish was one of the most critical factors for Miller's. While channel catfish can grow as large as 20 pounds, Jr. Miller would only accept fish that, after being dressed, would weigh in at about five ounces—a typical one-pound catfish dinner included three to four fish. He had experimented with larger fish but found that they required additional time in the fryers that resulted in the exterior being over-cooked—the fish had to be a split-tail channel catfish and it had to be a specific size—period!

In 1972 a severe drought in Florida adversely affected the catfish population and the Stokes Fishery began to compromise Miller's quality standards. They shipped fish of all sizes and, a wide range of species— including bullheads that had a distinctively different taste when prepared.

When Jr.'s protests had no impact on the quality of the shipments, he felt he had no choice but to search for an alternate supplier who would be willing to hold to his quality demands; it was then that fate met opportunity for an Illinois fish broker.

Don Dixon was President of Dixon Fisheries in East Peoria, Illinois. He had been told about Miller's and its growing business by his Florida contacts, but had felt that a single restaurant account did not hold enough potential to travel the distance to Colfax, a distance that would probably have also made Miller's difficult to service. He'd decided he might call on them if he was ever in the area. In 1972, Dixon signed a fresh catfish distribution agreement with a grocery chain. All but one of their stores were in the Chicago area, with the remaining store located in Indianapolis. Shortly after the contract was signed, Dixon was traveling with his salesman to make a call on the manager of the chain's Indianapolis location. As the two traveled down U.S. 52, Dixon spotted the sign to Colfax and directed his salesman to turn onto the angled county road leading into town.

After pulling up alongside the restaurant, Dixon entered the restaurant through the kitchen door and announced to the staff that, "I sell catfish and I hear you're having trouble with your fish. I'm here to solve your problems." Don Dixon admitted that at the time he had no idea Miller's had been at odds with their Florida source; it was simply his standard introduction to any new prospect he contacted. He also confessed his confidence was not high when one of the kitchen staff commented, "Just what we need, another damn catfish salesman." However, he pressed on and was pointed into the restaurant where he found Jr. Miller; Mike Miller had joined the business by the time declining fish quality had become an issue.

Dixon sat down with Jr. and Mike and enthusiastically proposed what the Dixon Fisheries could do for Miller's. The Dixon Fishery was in the business of distributing fresh, pond-raised catfish out of Mississippi—it was the first objection Dixon had to overcome. Jr. Miller was a firm believer that "native" catfish were the only type that had the distinctive flavor his customers had grown accustomed to. After being assured that people could tell no difference between farm raised fish and native catfish, Jr. continued to grill Dixon on what he could do that was better than Miller's current suppliers. Dixon simply guaranteed his catfish: they would be delivered on time, they would be exactly the specified size and, if they didn't meet Jr.'s standards, he would simply have to throw them in a freezer and Dixon would pick them up and return them for credit.

Jr. excused himself from the meeting and went to a telephone out of earshot of Don Dixon. He called the Stokes Fisheries and again protested the quality of his most recent shipment of fish. The voice on the other end indicated that if Miller's didn't want the fish that, because of the supply shortage, Stokes had a number of people who did. Jr. Miller told the man that those people could now have his entire supply—Stokes was to send no more fish to Colfax.

He returned to the table and asked Dixon to reconfirm his promises. After confirming each detail, Jr. told Dixon that he would take a shipment the following Monday. It was Wednesday and Dixon was confidant the shipment of a typical restaurant order, usually 100 pounds or less, could be put together exactly as specified. Dixon had neglected to ask about one small detail as he laid out his company's promises: how much fish did Miller's actually need? It was mid-summer and Miller's peak season. When Don Dixon was told that Miller's would need 3,000 pounds delivered by 9:00 A.M. on Monday, he had to grip the edge of the table to avoid falling from his chair. Dixon had less than five days to arrange a shipment of fish that exceeded most of his large grocery store chain's requirements.

Don Dixon pledged that the fish would be in Colfax on time. He excused himself and walked across the street to Colfax's only pay telephone to call his brother back at the Dixon offices in East Peoria. Dixon's brother first thought the call was a prank; he told Don, "There's no restaurant that's going to take 3,000 pounds of fresh catfish a week." Once Don Dixon convinced his brother that Miller's did, the two set about arranging for the shipment. At 9:00 a.m. the following Monday, a refrigerated truck containing 3,000 pounds of perfect, pond-raised "split-tail" catfish was sitting along the Oakland Street side of Miller's ready to be unloaded. The inaugural load launched a business association that endured for nearly twenty-five years.

Like many others, Don Dixon had his own take on why Miller's was successful. "You could never visit the place when at least two of the Miller family weren't there. Jr. and Mary Ellen in the beginning, then Mike and Beckie during the last twenty-five years. Customers like that kind of attention, they just feel things are being done right when the owners are there all the time." The Millers lost their valued supplier and close friend before the completion of this book. Don Dixon, the man who had burst onto the scene to "solve your problems", died April 25, 2002. For the Millers, Don Dixon not only solved their problems, he provided years of cherished friendship.

Chapter Six

"Number ninety-seven...your table is ready."

Jr. Miller has often been quoted, "I don't care if the governor showed up, he wasn't going to get in ahead of anybody." It was this uncompromising policy that made for the orderly flow of patrons through Miller's. By the late '50s, Miller's was hosting crowds on weekend nights that exceeded the population of Colfax; it was not uncommon on summer weekends or Purdue football Saturdays for customers to be waiting well past 11:00 p.m. for an available table. Why people were willing to wait—a wait that would often extend beyond an hour—is the underpinning of Miller's success.

That fried catfish would be responsible for bringing a steady stream of people to the little town of Colfax is incongruous. Yet Miller's Restaurant went from serving sixty pounds of fish on a weekend night in 1947, to serving over three thousand pounds a week during the peak summer months. While customer consumption drastically increased, the special care that went into preparing the catfish for the fryers remained unchanged. Rather than prepare six or seven hundred pounds of fish prior to opening each late afternoon, the fish were encased in the feather light cornmeal coating on demand. Orders were called out by Miller's waitresses and then conveyed via an intercom system to the kitchen. The kitchen staff, including ladies like Pearl Lenehan and Dorothy Haag, would prepare the fish 10 pounds at time. Bus boys carrying trays heaped with fish would often have to fight their way through the waiting customers who lined the wall from the kitchen to the fryers; a busy weekend night would often require the boys to make over 100 trips.

A typical Saturday night at Miller's.

Jr. Miller was a virtuoso at his craft. His ability to know precisely when to bring the fish up from the boiling oil made for a consistently tasty dish. Customers sitting at the short counter directly behind the fryers marveled at how he would bring up baskets of blazing hot catfish and with a quick squeeze with his bare fingers know the fish were cooked to perfection. Miller's method of preparing catfish had begun to create a following that found itself occasionally overwhelmed with cravings for the restaurant's special menu. The Millers cannot recollect the names of four Chicago bankers who would come through the door about every three months but the bankers had become addicted to Miller's. When their cravings got the best of them, they would charter a plane at Chicago's Meigs Field, fly to the Purdue University airport, rent a car then make the thirty-minute drive to Colfax. After gorging themselves with catfish and onion rings, they would travel back to West Lafayette and fly back to Chicago with their cravings satisfied for another ninety days.

Catfish made Miller's famous, but it might have been the onion rings that made them a legend. When queried, many people admitted they traveled to Colfax for the onion rings as much as the deep-fried catfish. A web of onions was immersed in a container of pale yellow batter, held for a split second above the batter, and then carefully immersed into a bath of bubbling oil. In just minutes the tangle of onions would be transformed into golden brown halos of delicious eating, a delicacy that earned a reputation early on. Henry Butler in his June 30, 1958 *Indianapolis Times* column, *The World's A Stage*, described Miller's as "that remarkable establishment," and the onion rings as, "among the noblest delicacies ever contrived by man's ingenuity."

While staff members like Ermadine Lawler had developed a deft touch at carefully immersing the batter-drenched onions into the fryer and then knowing the precise moment to rescue them from the hot grease, the addition of a new piece of equipment helped Miller's ensure that all deep-fried meals would always be cooked to perfection. Jr. had seen a deep fryer apparatus that utilized a large auger, approximately eight inches in diameter, installed in a trough that held 80 pounds of hot grease. Onions were coated and then slid into one end of the auger trough. The rings were slowly nudged along, eventually being lifted from the fryer at the opposite end of the trough. The consistent auger speed ensured that the rings remained in the grease for the precise amount of time.

The auger did present a problem for Ermadine Lawler; it had made her feel unnecessary in the creation of one of Miller's signature dishes. She requested a transfer to another part of the restaurant's operation—she wasn't going to spend her evenings simply watching onion rings curl through hot grease. The auger had rendered her magic touch insignificant and

Sandy Colter prepares Miller's onion rings, once described as, "among the noblest delicacies ever contrived by man's
ingenuity."

served as an early example of humans being replaced by technology. All of Miller's deep fried menu items, other than catfish, were prepared in the auger fryer. Although it cost over $5,000 to install, Jr. Miller felt the investment in the additional equipment paid off handsomely by guaranteeing cooking consistency and quality. The augered fryer was not used for catfish—it wasn't needed. From his early days of igniting splashed grease on an old coal-fired stove Jr. Miller had developed a feel for just how long the catfish should remain submerged, a feel that rivaled any mechanical timing device.

The onions and catfish, combined with a unique slaw and the early addition of Broasted® chicken and fried shrimp coalesced into a menu that, from the late 1940s on was unique to the Indiana restaurant scene. Miller's evolved from having no printed menu, to a small typed piece of paper to finally, a menu was printed on card stock in 1954. However, even when the printed menu appeared, Jr. Miller kept the nightly offering to a minimum.

"I couldn't see adding a bunch of other stuff when 85 percent of the people were going to order fish. People would waste a waitress' time reading all the other stuff and end up ordering fish anyway. It would have slowed things down too much to have any more on the menu than we did."

As limited as the Miller's menu may have been, the Miller family was always fielding requests for how they prepared their food, often with substantial offers of remuneration if they would divulge their secrets. A Phoenix women, and restaurant owner, was visiting friends in Indianapolis and the group had made the trip to Colfax. After finishing their meal, the woman came into the bar and sat at the counter. She had removed a business check from her purse and was filling it out as she talked to Jr. about the secret to his onion rings. The woman asked him how much it would take for him to give her his recipe—she was poised to enter the amount on the check that had been made out to Miller's Restaurant. Jr. didn't answer and the woman began establishing a range—would it take $5,000? $10,000? She seemed prepared to enter any amount Jr. asked. She finally filled out the check for $5,000 and placed it on the counter. Jr. looked at the check without comment. Finally he told the lady that the recipe had been part of his business for too many years to sell it now. He handed the check back to the woman who folded it, tore it in half and deposited it into a wastebasket. After complimenting Jr. on the evening's meal the group left the restaurant.

All of the recipes for Miller's signature dishes remain closely guarded. They were transferred when the business was sold and became the property of the new owner. About the only time Jr. Miller came close to divulging any of his trade secrets was in a letter to two men in Florida who had inquired about the preparation of Miller's catfish. The men had speculated about the recipe for the light coating that was applied prior to slipping the

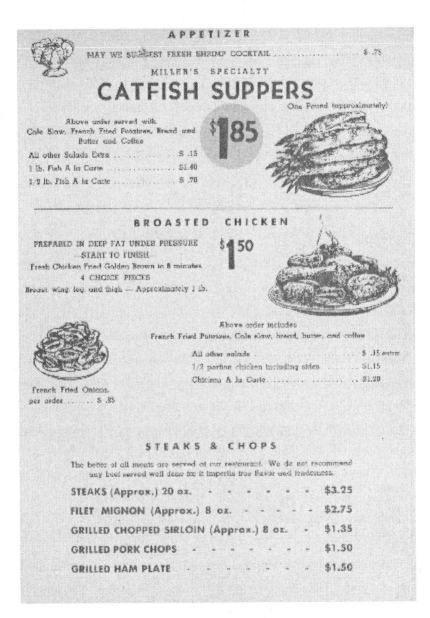

Miller's Restaurant's first "official" menu—1954.

FRENCH FRIED SHRIMP $1.50

8 FANTAILS

Above order includes:
French Fried Potatoes, Cole slaw, bread, butter, and coffee
All other salads . . . . $ .15 extra

SALADS

Pineapple and Cottage Cheese Salad. . . . . $ .25

Bean Salad . . . . $ .25

Macaroni . . . . $ .25

Combination Salad
   with choice of dressing . . . . $ .25

French Dressing, Mayonnaise, Vinegar and Oil, Garlic, and Bleu Cheese

DESSERTS

Fresh Strawberry Short Cake and Whipped Cream . . . . $ .40

Fresh Strawberry Sundae . . . . $ .25

Vanilla Ice Cream . . . . $ .10 and .20

Chocolate Ice Cream   Strawberry Ice Cream   Lime Sherbet
Pineapple Sherbet   Raspberry Salad

BEVERAGES

Coffee . . . . $ .05

Milk—White, Chocolate, or Buttermilk . . . . . . $ .10

Ice Tea . . . . $ .10

Lemonade . . . . $ .10

Coke . . . . $ .10

7-up . . . . $ .10

Pepsi Cola . . . . $ .10

Free Parking
FOR
MILLER'S CUSTOMERS
AT SHELL STATION

BEER
WE WILL TRY TO HAVE
YOUR FAVORITE BRAND

Please pay your waitress and we hope to serve you again in the near future.

95

fish into the cooking oil. Jr. told the men they were on the right track without saying they had discovered his secret. He did reveal in the letter that one secret was making sure the fryer was large enough to not crowd the fish as they cooked. He also emphasized his belief that the consistent cooking temperature maintained with electric fryers had been superior to his experience with gas-fired equipment. Beyond that, no recipe ever escaped the Miller vaults even though hundreds of customers have attempted to replicate them in their home kitchens.

As simple as it was, the restaurant's menu put Colfax on the map and began to be a way of life in Colfax. Children born in Colfax after 1950 often had to grow to become adults and travel outside their home community to realize that surf and turf wasn't catfish and broasted chicken—it had been all they knew growing up. As crowds grew, local residents had to develop strategies for enjoying Miller's fare. They knew it was best to visit the restaurant during weekday nights or simply utilize the Miller's carry out service. Many in the surrounding area went years without ever being seated in the restaurant while still maintaining a steady diet of catfish, onion rings, slaw, chicken and fried shrimp.

The Millers invested very few dollars in advertising after its first few years. They discovered they had created effective advertising in the word-of-mouth endorsements that were bringing a steady flow of new customers to Colfax. Jr. Miller makes no apologies for his lack of self-promotion, "You can't beat the credibility that comes from someone telling someone else about your place. We just felt like our customers were creating all the advertising we needed."

Miller's was not a place to come if you were looking for a quiet evening out. In many restaurants the constant din of a Saturday night crowd might have been annoying for some people, but it was part of going to Colfax.

The noise and hilarity that emanated from the gathered throng of people was the trademark of a place people visited because it was fun to be among people having fun. It made it easy for people to recommend Miller's to their family and friends—it was rare that first time visitors didn't become steady customers.

Customers who had experienced the delight of Miller's catfish enjoyed bringing newcomers to the restaurant, many of whom were reticent about the prospect of eating a fish that was often perceived as a "garbage" fish in other parts of the country. Harry Bradway, long time Lafayette sports broadcaster and founding father of the Colt baseball World Series in Lafayette, would often bring officials from the Colt League offices in Pennsylvania to Miller's during the tournament. After convincing them they should sample the catfish, he would watch closely to measure their reaction. Bradway relates, "It was rare that these people didn't request a trip to Miller's when they returned to Lafayette for the next year's World Series."

As crowds began to grow people became accustomed to lengthy waits, particularly on summer weekends or Purdue football weekends. They would come to Colfax equipped with playing cards and folding chairs to sit out on the sidewalk in order to hear their number being broadcast out to the street. "Doc" Davis' liquor store would see a steady stream of customers who would purchase six packs of cold beer to help pass the time. The Millers recollect that card playing wasn't the only way customers passed the time waiting for a table.

One story ranks as one of the most creative and amorous ways of passing time while waiting for a table at Miller's. A couple from Indianapolis arrived one evening and found the wait for a table had reached nearly an hour. The lady, an employee of an Indianapolis department store, entered the bar, leaned over the counter and motioned for Jr. to step closer to the bar. She whispered in his ear to ask if there was a condom machine in the men's restroom. After informing her there wasn't, he smiled and reached under the counter. Removing a small package from the supply he maintained for his waitresses, he discreetly pushed the package toward the lady. From that evening, whenever the couple visited Miller's and the wait was to extend beyond forty-five minutes, the lady would ask Jr. for a "package" and the couple would travel outside of Colfax to seek out a convenient barn. Upon pulling into the barn, the couple would put the condom to its intended use and then return to town just in time to hear their number being called.

In its first years of business, Miller's had begun to set the standard for how its customers judged other restaurants. Some other establishments apparently didn't measure up. W. Paul Sullivan sent a postcard to the Millers, dated 12/19/64; Anthony's Restaurant in San Diego, California had provided the postcard. The postcard touted the restaurant to be "world famous for gourmet fish delicacies". Mr. Sullivan didn't appear to agree with the restaurant's billing. The message he wrote on the card read, "If any of your cooks should be in the San Diego area, please have them call on these people and show them how to fry fish. Compared to Miller's, their fish stink!"

There were no bigger fans of the Indianapolis 500® than Beulah and Maurice (Pat) Cripe, who were both employed at Miller's; Beulah Cripe for over twenty years. They would make the hour-long trip to the track every day in May and, although Jr. Miller was an avid race fan, the Cripes would rush back to Colfax in order to arrive at the restaurant on time—Jr. was not so avid a race fan as to excuse tardiness.

Beulah Cripe was never bashful when it came to approaching her racing idols. Her effusive nature, lightning quick smile and uproarious laugh allowed her to slide past many a security guard during her visits to the race

Pat and Beulah Cripe

track. Once inside and among the drivers and crews, she was an enthusiastic ambassador for Miller's.

One of the first drivers she met and convinced to make the drive to Colfax was Bobby Grim. Grim had earned recognition as Rookie of the Year when he qualified in the middle of the second row for the 1959 race and had become one of the Cripe's favorite drivers. Beulah and Pat Cripe became good friends with Bobby and Betty Grim and invited them to Miller's. After their first visit, the Grims became steady customers, often bringing carloads of other drivers and their wives from the track. Betty Grim remembers their visits to Miller's with great fondness, "It was only a six-pack from Indianapolis."

Her husband would often plan a trip to Colfax, being cautious to not let others around the garage in on his plan. "If people found out we were going to Miller's, we'd have four or five carloads," Betty Grim said. "All I know is that we fell in love with the place the first time we went up. They (the Millers) were such race fans. Jr. would send Bobby cigars or a bottle of

L to R: Bobby Grim, Betty Grim, Al Sweeney (IMCA)

champagne after a race. They just made you feel important; they treated us like royalty."

One of the couples who would often make the trip to Colfax with the Grims was Johnny and Betty Rutherford. Johnny Rutherford, three-time champion of the Indianapolis 500®, remembers his trips to Miller's. "There was simply no place like it. There were other catfish places, but Miller's was just a special place. The first time Bobby and Betty took us up there, we were hooked." Rutherford was always among a group that traveled to Colfax with former IMCA (International Motor Contest Association) president Al Sweeney. Sweeney would often take groups of his "boys", all veterans of the IMCA circuit, to Miller's every year during their month-long stay in Indianapolis in May. "There'd be ten or fifteen of us every trip, but we could sit there and talk about racing and we'd never be bothered, even though the place was always packed. I know we always had to wait for a table," Rutherford said.

Some associated with racing didn't believe the "everyone waits" philosophy was so ironclad. Sal Fish, CEO of SCORE International Off Road Racing, was Publisher of *Hot Rod Magazine* in 1974. Based in California, Fish made several trips to Colfax during his stays in Indianapolis for the Indianapolis 500® and the NHRA® drag racing championships in September. He'd learned from earlier trips to Colfax that it was impossible to get a table ahead of anyone. Early one evening he called to ensure that Mary Ellen Miller was working the "number line"; he was going to bring up a special visitor who, as Fish said, "never waited on a table in any restaurant anywhere in the world".

Upon their arrival, Mary Ellen handed the men a number and informed them there would be a forty-five minute wait. Fish's guest pulled a money clip from his pocket and offered a gratuity if they could be seated right away; Mary Ellen again told the guest it would be a forty-five minute wait and she would call their number when it came up. The men walked back to their car to wait for the number to be called. The guest grew impatient after only a five-minute wait and returned back to the restaurant. Another five minutes passed and Fish's guest returned to the car—Sal Fish had not informed the man of the identity of the demure lady they had encountered upon their entrance to the restaurant—he had calculated that his guest would find out soon enough. Upon his return, Fish queried his guest as to the status of the wait; he assumed he knew what the answer would be. He didn't know how much the man had offered Mary Ellen Miller for immediate seating, but his guest said that upon offering it, he was told, "Keep your money, I own the place." As promised, the men were seated approximately thirty minutes later. Sal Fish's guest, George Hurst, President of the Hurst Shifter Company, had finally found the restaurant in the world that had made him wait for a table.

Sal Fish was also one of Miller's greatest racing ambassadors. He would bring many of the most famous names in racing to Miller's during his trips to Indiana, including one evening during the drag racing championships for an impromptu bachelor party prior to his marriage to his fiancée, a native of Fort Wayne, Indiana. Sal Fish has traveled throughout the world and dined in a number of the world's best restaurants, but, when contacted at his home in Malibu, California, he read from a Miller's menu he'd taken from a kitchen drawer. "I've been in a lot of places, but this is the only menu I've ever asked to keep. In all my travels, I never found a place that had the combination of great food and personality as Miller's; it simply was one of a kind," Fish said.

Another frequent visitor to Miller's who often caused a stir among the crowd whenever he entered the restaurant, was Richard Afflis, better known as "Dick the Bruiser". Afflis, who earned the reputation as "the World's Most Dangerous Wrestler", would often come to Miller's on his return to Indianapolis from visiting the grave of his father in Delphi, Indiana. He was accompanied on most visits by his wife Louise, and mother, Mrs. Margaret Afflis Johnson. According to Louise Afflis, "We just loved going there. Dick could just blend into the crowd and have a quiet evening. Unlike when we'd try and go out around Indianapolis, people at Miller's knew who Dick was, but they left him alone. I think James (Jr.) had a lot to do with that."

The Bruiser's visits were most often uneventful. However, according to an item in Irving Leibowitz's column in the *Indianapolis Times*, Margaret Afflis Johnson departed the restaurant one evening to discover she had lost a diamond ring valued at $1,500. Meda Phebus, who was on social security and working part-time at Miller's, found the ring shortly after the group's departure. By the time Richard Afflis called the restaurant, Jr. Miller reported that the ring had been discovered. However, there was one incident more noteworthy than a lost ring.

Richard Afflis drove into Colfax late one evening to find only one parking space within three blocks of Miller's; the space was across the street from the direction he had entered town. After making a u-turn and guiding his car into the space, Afflis slid from the driver's seat to find the Colfax town marshal, Charles Banta, standing by the driver's side door. Charlie Banta served two roles for the town of Colfax; he was the town's chief law enforcement office and he was also in charge of street maintenance. He most often was dressed for his role as street commissioner, which typically was a uniform of blue jeans and a red and black plaid, flannel shirt; it was the attire he sported as he confronted The Bruiser. As Street Commissioner, Banta was noted for his fairness in allocating the town's skimpy budget by keeping the repairs equitably distributed among all residents of Colfax. Rather than utilize the town's budget for street repairs for only selected streets, and ignoring the repair needs of some streets completely, he would estimate the repair needs of the entire town and compare it to the available budget dollars. One year he discovered that street repairs would require a budget nearly double of what had been allocated for the year. He felt it unfair to ignore half the streets in town and proceeded to repair every other pothole along every street in Colfax, ensuring that all residents had been allocated their fair share of the town's street repair budget.

Charlie Banta was not known for his tact. It's not known whether he was familiar with the out-of-town driver who had just violated the "no u-turn" rule of Colfax, but whether he did or not, he was quick to accost Afflis about his indiscretion. The collision of two strong wills most often leads to an escalated confrontation. Banta had made one tactical error in that he had not identified himself as the town marshal and, instead, looked very much like any man on the street who had been assigned to fix potholes. After tolerating a few minutes of Banta's harangue, Afflis reached out, gathered the lapels of Banta's plaid flannel shirt and lifted the short, stocky man straight up from the street to a point where he was staring Banta straight in the eye. As he dangled in mid-air, Banta's flannel shirt opened to reveal the badge he had pinned to the work shirt under the flannel shirt. Seeing the badge, Afflis slowly lowered the stunned man back to the street. Banta did not say a word after being placed back down and watched as Afflis, his wife, and mother disappeared into the restaurant.

Entering the barroom section of the restaurant, Afflis immediately approached the counter in front of the fryers where Mike Miller was stationed. Afflis told Mike that he had to have a table immediately, preferably in the back room of the restaurant. He explained the confrontation that had occurred on the street in front of the business and, that he was sure the local law enforcement officer was calling for back up as they spoke; Afflis was certain that a swarm of state police would be entering the restaurant seeking him out for arrest. No such sweep occurred, but Afflis and his guests ordered and ate their dinner in less than thirty minutes before making a hasty get-away from Colfax in the evening darkness.

Other than the one encounter with Colfax's law enforcement, the Millers always saw a different side of Richard Afflis. According to Mike Miller, "People only knew him from what they saw on television. We saw a polite and gracious man who treated our people with great respect; we lost a great friend when Dick passed away." Possibly because of Afflis' affinity for Miller's, a number of professional wrestlers were often found dining at the restaurant during their barnstorming trips around Indiana. The myths of professional wrestling were often exploded for the young boys of Colfax as they gaped through the windows of Miller's to get a glimpse of their favorite mat stars. It was difficult for youngsters to comprehend how men who behaved as mortal enemies in the ring were now squeezed into one of the barroom booths acting as if they were long lost brothers. Ring performers Wilbur Snyder, Yukon Eric, Wladek "Killer" Kowalski (who had supposedly bitten one of Yukon Eric's ears off during a match), and Dr. Bill Miller were often spotted enjoying a meal in relative obscurity among the Miller's regulars.

Purdue University proved to be a major source of business for Miller's and was instrumental in establishing their reputation both nationally and internationally. Purdue students began finding their way to Colfax in the early '50s and, by the time the Millers sold their business, many former Purdue students were escorting their grandchildren to Colfax to introduce them to the treasure they'd discovered during their college days. It took only ten years for the Millers to discover how far reaching the Purdue influence could be. In 1957, profits from the business had been enough to save the money necessary for Jr. Miller to send Ralph and Irene Ashley overseas. He wanted his father and mother-in-law to revisit the sites where Ralph Ashley had served during World War I and, most importantly, the gravesite of their fallen son. Ralph Ashley never missed an opportunity to promote his son-in-law's business. While visiting a London restaurant, he pulled a pack of matches from his pocket with the trademark Miller's catfish on the front. The owner of the restaurant visited the Ashley's table and picked up the matchbook. He examined it closely and proceeded to describe "downtown" Colfax in detail. The owner's son was a student at Purdue and had taken his father to Colfax during his visit to the United States the previous summer. In the early '60s the Millers began sending Christmas cards to people who had signed a guest register during their visit to the restaurant; the first year's mailing included addresses in all fifty states and seven foreign countries.

Purdue students weren't the only ones who frequented Miller's. The university hosted an array of business conferences throughout the year and several groups returned to Purdue because they discovered attendance would often be positively affected when program participants knew that a trip to Miller's could be worked into the program agenda. One such group, the Plumbers and Pipefitters Union would hold their annual conference on the Purdue campus. Each year the conference was held, more and more of the attendees would come to Colfax, finally growing to as many as sixty people. Some would come more than one night during their stay in West Lafayette. Purdue managed to cost the Miller's the group's business when the university decided to hire non-union labor for a campus construction project and the group ultimately moved their annual meeting to the University of Michigan.

Purdue's greatest contribution to Miller's customer counts usually occurred when the Boilermaker football team played at Ross-Ade Stadium. The staff would listen to home games on the radio and after the final second ticked off knew that in less than sixty minutes the population of Colfax would more than double over the next six hours. While good for business, the football crowds presented a crowd control issue for the Millers. Most fans were well behaved, but after several hours of tailgating some would arrive in an unruly mood. The weekend the staff dreaded most was when the Indiana University Hoosiers came to West Lafayette. The restaurant would fill with a blend of fans from both camps and it was not uncommon for heated verbal exchanges to break out in the middle of the dining room and, in some instances, hand-to-hand combat on the adjacent sidewalks. The Millers reverted back to Raleigh Higer's peace-keeping days by hiring off-duty policemen to ensure the crowd stayed under control.

There was any number of reasons why it was impossible to "influence" your way to an early seating at Miller's. The first reason sprang from Jr. Miller's business acumen—it simply accelerated the turns for each table. The second, and most fundamental reason was philosophical. Jr. Miller made no differentiation in the status of his customers—they were each cherished—all were equal no matter their position in life. Farmers and construction workers were comfortable dining alongside doctors and lawyers. Bob Higman remembers climbing off his corn picker after a long day of harvesting and bringing his entire work crew to Colfax from his farm near Romney. "In the early '50s we'd come in dressed in our overalls and Jr. and Mary Ellen would treat us like we were the most important customers who'd walked in that night; it's one of the biggest reasons they were so successful; they loved their customers with a passion." Beginning in 1955, Higman went from his corn picker to parlay his love of motor racing into a distinguished career. He was elected to the Midget Racing Hall of Fame in 1995, being recognized as one of the most accomplished engine and chassis designers in professional racing. He was among the first in the racing profession to discover the allure of Miller's. Early on, as he began to establish his name in the racing world, Higman brought a young driver to Miller's who had traveled to Indiana and agreed to work on Higman's farm in exchange for the opportunity to drive Higman's high-powered midget racecars. The young driver, A.J. Foyt, visited Miller's many times after his introduction to Miller's food and atmosphere.

For some, Miller's food was not the primary attraction. Rick Albrecht first learned of Miller's in the late '60s from business associates in Indianapolis. By the early 1970s he was traveling to Miller's with an entourage that would sometimes number 20 people. Albrecht had been involved in various aspects of commercial development in Indianapolis, but was enticed to open a restaurant in 1974. Since then, he has owned and operated 19 restaurants, including the popular Rick's Cafe Boatyard on Eagle Creek Reservoir. "I didn't really go to Colfax for the food, even though it was very good. We went to Miller's because it was simply fun to go there. You knew you were going to get great food and arguably the best service anywhere. The Millers always provided a great setting for us to have as much fun as any place we could go; I always marveled at how good their service would be."

Miller's never officially provided dining entertainment, but it was not unusual for impromptu floor shows to unfold. One evening several members of the world-renowned Purdue Glee Club traveled to Colfax. As they were completing their meal, the group's waitress joked that they might receive a discount on their meal if they would perform a number for the assembled crowd. The group stood and launched into a musical program that lasted nearly 30 minutes. The seated diners were delighted by the show—the customers who remained waiting for open tables weren't as enamored with the young men's performance. As the waitress had hinted, the group was provided with complimentary dinners for their performance. Local television personality, and Mulberry, Indiana resident, Curley Myers also provided extemporaneous entertainment along with his group, The Shady Acres Band; the group included Bob Harshman, Bob Coapstick, Keith Kallner, Carl Lambert, and Nancy Porter. One evening they were returning from an engagement when they decided to stop at Miller's shortly before closing. Jr. asked Myers, who had been a high school classmate, if the group would bring in their instruments and play a few selections; as with the Glee Club, Myers' group sang for their suppers.

With success came a reputation that was beginning to reach throughout Indiana and the Midwest. In the early 1960s the notoriety of the little catfish restaurant in Colfax created a critical test of Jr. Miller's "all customers are equal" philosophy. One Saturday night in the summer of 1964, two cars pulled into Colfax and parked alongside the restaurant. The four occupants in each car entered and approached Mary Ellen Miller to announce they were members of the NAACP in Gary, Indiana and expected to be seated immediately. As was the case every Saturday night in the summer, all tables had filled up and numbers were being distributed to customers. Mary Ellen explained the seating policy and assured them they would be called the moment a table for eight came available. She invited the group to have a seat in the interior waiting area or, if they wanted, they could wait outside, explaining that the loudspeaker system could be heard out on the street; the group chose to stand only six feet from Mary Ellen until their number was called.

After a twenty-minute wait, Mary Ellen announced a number that was higher than the number she had given the group from Gary. One of the group members, stepping back among the tables of the original dining room so as to be heard by as many diners as possible, loudly protested that his group had assumed they would be passed over in favor of white patrons. Mary Ellen calmly explained that the higher numbers were for tables seating two and four diners and that she needed to have two adjacent tables open so they could be combined to accommodate the group of eight. She invited the spokesman to look into the main dining room at an empty table that was being saved for their group and she explained that they would be seated as soon as either one of the adjacent tables was vacated. Within five minutes the second table came open and the group was seated without incident.

A group of local residents were in the bar area and had observed the confrontation. When they saw the group was being seated, some protested to Jr. that he shouldn't be serving "those kind" in Colfax. One man was coarse enough to suggest that if he served the group that Colfax would be "crawling with niggers" in no time; the patron was unfortunate enough to be sitting within arm's reach of Jr. Miller. He quickly found his shirt in the grasp of a powerful hand and was within a few inches of being pulled over the counter onto the floor in front of the fryers. Jr. stopped short of pulling the man over the bar, but after shoving him back onto the stool, told the man he had two options for leaving the restaurant—either through the door or the plate glass window. Four others in the bar followed the man out the door and never returned to Miller's; it was business Jr. Miller never regretted losing.

Colfax's population of predominantly white, blue-collar workers had a well-documented history of intolerance. A 1930 edition of the *Clinton County Review*, edited at the time by Warren C. Bowers, reported an incident on then, State Road 52, involving a car carrying six "buck niggers". By 1933, the newspaper had tempered its description of African-Amercians slightly by referring to them as "coloreds", but the Colfax PTA continued to sponsor a yearly minstrel show with local businessmen in blackface and "shades of Aunt Jemima". Jr. Miller did not participate in the shows, which were discontinued in 1953. Schuyler Colfax may not have been proud of the incident in the town that bore his name, but he would have no doubt applauded one of the town's leading businessmen who was carrying on the former Vice President's battle against racial discrimination.

In subsequent months, three more groups traveled to Colfax from the Calumet Region of Indiana, each time testing the system. When it became clear the Millers held true to their philosophy that all customers were equal, no matter who you were or the color of your skin, the confrontations stopped. Over the following years a number of the original groups who had first come to prove Jr. Miller a racist, traveled back to Colfax to patronize a restaurant they found to be as friendly and accommodating as any in the state.

With hundreds of people waiting in line and the appearance of luxurious living that a swimming pool and color televisions created, Miller's Restaurant appeared to be a gold mine. It also became a target for some of the more unsavory characters in the surrounding areas and their after hours criminal pursuits. The business had not experienced any burglaries during its first twenty years of operation. Then, two robberies occurred in a three-week period in late December 1966 and early January 1967 that prompted the installation of a silent alarm wired to both Jr.'s and Mike Miller's homes. The first test of the system came one early morning on May 10, 1967. Being awakened by the alarm, both men, along with Mary Ellen Miller rushed to the restaurant. Mary Ellen remained outside the restaurant while the two men, both armed, entered the restaurant. Assuming the perpetrator was aware he had been discovered and was hiding somewhere in the building, the Millers began to search the premises. Mike discovered two men hiding behind a stack of beer cases in a back storeroom. By the time of Mike's discovery, Colfax town marshal Charlie Banta had arrived on the crime scene.

After flushing the two bandits from their hiding place, Mary Ellen Miller entered the storeroom. Even though they had not appeared to be carrying weapons, one of the burglars made a threatening remark about harming her. Mike cocked the large caliber handgun he was holding and the men fell silent. After herding the two into the main barroom, one of the burglars shouted he was leaving and "would kill the old man" doing it, referring to Banta, as he ran toward the corner door of the barroom. As he reached the door, Jr. Miller fired the 16-gauge shotgun he held over the burglar's head. The blast shattered the glass of the main window, showering the burglar in shards of glass and shotgun pellets. Covered in blood, the burglar fell to the floor, finally convinced that Jr. Miller's next shot would be a direct hit. As the man fell to the floor, Clinton County sheriff's deputies arrived and arrested both burglars who were from Frankfort, but were living in the Capitol Hotel in Lafayette.

After his conviction, the Millers received a hand-written letter from the 21-year-old burglar who had been shot in the robbery attempt. The letter, sent from prison where he was serving a 2-5 year sentence for the break-in, expressed remorse for his crime and thanked the Millers for sparing him. He went on to pledge that, upon his release, he would never commit another crime. After his release from prison, the man entered public life and worked in the building trades. Although he died at the age of 44, the man followed through with his vow of remaining a law-abiding citizen.

Not all criminals who broke into Miller's were brought to justice. Four years had elapsed from the May 1967 break-in when the silent alarm was triggered in the early morning of May 12, 1971. The Millers went through the drill they had practiced for break-ins, covering each of the three possible exits of the restaurant. Entering the building Jr. Miller discovered two young men in their late teens standing in the small dining room behind the barroom. County sheriff's deputy Charles Haughs arrived and arrested the two burglars. Shortly after their arrests, a third man surrendered and the three were taken to Frankfort for booking. The following morning when Jr. Miller learned that the three had been released without bail he was livid. He called Judge Everett Lucas and expressed his concern that the three, all sons of prominent Thorntown residents, had been released and asked for an explanation. When Lucas told him that they had been released because they weren't guilty, Jr. Miller's anger grew to a boil. To have a judge declare three burglars who had been discovered after breaking in to his business not guilty was unfathomable.

Jr. Miller could not contain his anger. He composed a letter to the *Frankfort Times* and traveled to Frankfort to have his attorney, Tom Robinson, review the letter before submitting it to the newspaper. The letter was caustic, to a point where Robinson advised that it would probably lead to a contempt of court charge for Jr. Robinson deleted some of the more inflammatory language and told Jr. he was on his own. Jr. took the letter to the newspaper office and submitted it to the editor. After reviewing the letter, the editor said he would run it only if Judge Lucas reviewed it first and gave his permission. Jr. told the editor he'd wait at the newspaper office while he took it to Lucas for his "blessing". The editor returned indicating that Lucas had given his permission to run the letter. Jr. Miller's letter appeared in the newspaper exactly as he'd first written it, including all comments that had been purged from the letter by Tom Robinson. As scathing as the letter was, no repercussions were felt, probably because Jr. Miller's point had been difficult to refute.

Judge Lucas aside, the growth of the business brought Jr. Miller a level of political influence—influence he rarely wielded unless he felt he was being compromised. In 1964, Jr. learned that Frankfort resident and Colfax native, Kern Murray, had the intention of acquiring a beer license to open a tavern in Colfax. Murray and Colfax resident and high school classmate, Kizer Craven planned to remodel a property owned by Craven adjacent to the Colfax post office and only a few steps from Miller's front door. Murray and Craven had gained the support of their new venture from several local businessmen, including Lawrence Lake. Miller's had reduced their hours of operation in 1960 and had begun opening at 4:00 p.m., leaving the town dry until late afternoon and completely dry on Mondays when Miller's was closed. According to Murray, "Kizer and I thought we were doing Jr. a favor. With all the people waiting for a table, we thought it would give them someplace to wait. We were going to be close enough that people could still hear their number being called." Jr. Miller didn't see it that way; he was concerned that it would have a negative impact on the image of the business he'd worked so hard to develop. "I didn't want guys who had been drinking all afternoon stumbling into our place and disrupting things. I was sure it would drive business away."

According to Murray, he'd been assured that his liquor license would be approved, especially since he had the support of the influential businessmen who wanted to have a tavern in Colfax that opened by late morning; it turned out Jr. Miller had greater influence. Dr. Charles Skinner, a Colfax veterinarian, was president of the Colfax Town Board. He received a call from Jr. expressing his concern about Murray's pending application. After going to Skinner's home, the board president proceeded to poll the other board members via telephone to measure their opinion about the addition of another tavern in Colfax. After polling each member, Charles Skinner turned to Jr. and informed him that since the county liquor board would yield to the opinion of the local governing board there would be no additional licenses granted for new taverns in Colfax; F.M. Goldsberry would have no doubt been pleased with the decision.

After the initial shock of having had the liquor board renege on their pledge for a Colfax license, Murray purchased Frankfort's Coachlight Inn out of bankruptcy in 1967, a business he successfully operated until early 1978. Although he was disappointed in the board's action, he harbored no ill feelings toward Jr. Miller. "We got to be good friends over the years and I can't count how many times we went to Colfax to eat. It just surprised Kizer and me that Jr. was so against our plan."

A business in a town as small as Colfax relies heavily on well-placed signage along the roads leading to its front door. One October evening in 1972, a man called Miller's to order 18 catfish dinners, saying he would come by the restaurant to pick them up. He was calling from Lebanon and said he would arrive in less than 30 minutes. The dinners were prepared and waiting for the customer to arrive. After nearly an hour had passed, the customer called, explaining he had not been able to find Colfax. Jr. told the man to simply look for the large billboard pointing to the county road leading into town. The man told Jr. he had traveled up and down the road three times and had not seen a billboard.

Unbeknownst to the Millers, a local sign company had taken chain saws and flattened the sign earlier in the day. The 1971 Federal Highway Commission had ruled all billboards be at least 500 feet from the highway and any not in compliance were to be taken down. State Road 52 had been expanded to four lanes in the late '50s and given a U. S. highway designation, making it a target of the beautification act. After driving out to the highway and seeing his billboard laying flat in a farm field, Jr. Miller called State Representative Lucille Woofendale to protest.

Woofendale contacted U.S. Representative John Myers who immediately went to work negotiating a compromise to allow the Miller's billboard to stay. After three days, Myers was successful in working out a compromise—which really wasn't a compromise at all. The billboard was replaced immediately and a second large sign was erected well inside the 500-foot zone just five miles to the north on U.S. 52.

Miller's also occasionally encountered political problems in Colfax. While some businessmen like Earl Anderson benefited from the large crowds of people who frequented Miller's, others were not as enamored with the restaurant and the congestion crowds sometimes created in the center of town. Sam Birge, who owned the liquor store once operated by Doc Davis, solicited the Colfax Town Board to assign a reserved parking place in front of his store. He wanted the designated loading zone so his customers would not have to walk as far to his store, or in many cases, double-park in the street. The designated parking space was directly across from the bar entrance to Miller's. When informed of the request, Jr. Miller appeared at the town board meeting and indicated he would not give up the space. His rationale was that if Birge was awarded his parking space, every business in town would request a similar reserved space and ultimately every parking space around the restaurant would no longer be available to his customers. He also had another option in his back pocket. Miller's had never sold packaged liquor even though it held the license to do so. The decision had been made in deference to long-time employee June Davis, whose disabled husband ran the liquor store. The policy of no package liquor continued, even after the Davis' sold the store. Jr. Miller made it clear that if Sam Birge were granted the reserved space that Miller's would initiate the sale of package liquor. Birge immediately withdrew his request and the matter was dropped.

One of the most intriguing elements of the story of Miller's is how it managed to position itself with such a diverse and far-reaching clientele. By the early 1960s, residents of Colfax who traveled throughout the United States on business or vacations began to realize the impact Miller's was having in making Colfax famous. Colfax residents tell stories of traveling to Washington D.C., California, Texas, Canada and other places hundreds of miles from their little Indiana town to find people who were as familiar with Colfax as the restaurant owner Ralph and Irene Ashley had encountered in England. Rather than apologize for their small, out-of-the-way place, as some small towners sometimes do, Colfax residents found themselves enjoying near celebrity status because they lived where Miller's lived. When the end finally came, it made the last days of Miller's even harder to endure for many in Colfax.

Scott Robey

Chapter Seven

"It's best to play in our own backyard."

Miller's had reached the highest volume in its history as it entered the decade of the '70s. Out-of-town and out-of-state visitors had reached new levels, prompting a number of diners to suggest to the Millers that they consider expanding their restaurant concept to other, often larger cities. A number of Indianapolis businessmen approached the Millers about opening locations in the malls that were being constructed throughout Marion County. Other suggestions for expanding Miller's ranged as far as California, Las Vegas, Denver and the Deep South. Sal Fish urged the Miller's to consider opening a restaurant in Los Angeles, "I was positive it would have gone over huge out here. They told me they just wanted to do a good job in Colfax, so we never pursued it."

Al and Betty Harding started frequenting Miller's in 1965 from their home in Indianapolis. Al Harding remembers his first impression, "They were exceptionally nice people and we were really taken by that. The fact the food was outstanding just made the trip to Colfax fun to take." Harding, a commercial real estate developer and contractor approached Jr. Miller about the possibility of putting a Miller's in a property he was developing on the east side of Indianapolis. Harding went so far as to submit plans for what the restaurant might look like; the plans included a shake-covered canopy around the exterior of the building. While Jr. was flattered that Harding would suggest that a Miller's would be successful in Indianapolis, he was still reluctant to open a business he could not personally supervise on a daily basis. While he declined Harding's invitation, he did "borrow" the idea of adding the shake canopy around the building in Colfax. The construction of the canopy provided shelter for the long lines of people that continued to grow into the '70s.

There were a number of reasons Jr. Miller, and Mike Miller later on, resisted the temptation to take Miller's to other regional locations; the most basic was their small town orientation. The roots of the Miller family were deeply seated in small town living and it's where they wanted to remain. As was the case with his decision to not open another Miller's in Indianapolis with Al Harding, Jr. believed the "Miller's concept" would not work if he or Mike could not be part of the day-to-day operation; a belief that proved to be accurate after the business was sold in 1995. Jr. Miller believed that the success of his business was tied directly to his family's daily supervision and presence. Jr. worked hard to remember every one of his thousands of customers, but when names could not be put with faces, he developed his trademark greeting. Customers coming into the restaurant through the barroom entrance would most often be welcomed with, "Hiya neighbor!" The voice inflection of the greeting made everyone who entered feel as though they'd come to a good friend's home for dinner. But it was this part of the business that Jr. felt could never be replicated in a satellite operation. Finally acknowledging the impact of his daily presence, "I guess we always felt that even if we could teach people how to prepare the food, we could never teach them how to recreate the personality of our business, so we just decided there would always be just one Miller's."

By the early '50s a number of imitators, some by coincidence and others by design, began to crop up. Some contended that it was a coincidence, but a number of the imitators that began serving fried catfish were within a short driving distance of Colfax where the long lines had begun to form several years before. Restaurants in Clarks Hill, Thorntown, Cicero, Pittsboro, and Indianapolis all either added fried catfish to their menus or, if it was already included, began heavy promotion of the item. One Thorntown restaurant, the Hillhouse Cafe, promoted "Fresh channel catfish dinners" in a 1952 advertisement. The proprietors of the Hillhouse Cafe must have participated in the Miller's early experimentation before adding catfish to their own menu. The Hillhouse, besides their newly added catfish dinners, also promoted chop suey and chow mein specials; something Irene Ashley was no doubt flattered by since her son-in-law had chosen to not make her oriental specialties a full-time addition to his restaurant's menu. Other restaurants as far away as Cincinnati were advertising "Colfax-style" catfish in their newspaper advertising. If any in Colfax doubted that their small town had become synonymous with Miller's it was verified when legal opinions were rendered that "Colfax-style" was a direct reference to Miller's and, therefore a trademark infringement. The Millers were not so concerned about their trade name-borrowing competition as they were that the imitators could not measure up to their own quality standards and would cast an unfavorable shadow on the Miller's of Colfax reputation. There are those who might attempt to make the point that since the idea had come from Sam's in Pittsburg, Indiana, that Miller's itself was an imitator. However, as is often the case, it's not the idea, but the execution of the idea that matters. Miller's simply "out-Sam'd" Sam's. Most of the people who sampled the Miller's imitators conceded that Miller's was in a class by itself.

If the Millers had ever held any thoughts of expanding outside of Colfax, their one experience in big city food service most likely led them to abandon those thoughts. In 1973, the manager of the Indianapolis Athletic Club, Maurice Corya, sent an invitation to the Millers to participate in the club's "Taste of the Indiana" promotion. They were asked to serve Miller's catfish dinners to the club's patrons, which were to be prepared in the club's kitchen. Jr. Miller initially declined the invitation, skeptical that he and his staff could handle the assignment. Corya assured him that the evening would be relatively quiet since the Millers were scheduled to participate in the program on Monday of Thanksgiving week. Miller's had gone to a five night week a few years before and were available for the Monday night event. Corya estimated that, because of the nearby holiday, there would be no more than 60 dinners served; the Millers relented and agreed to participate.

A van was loaded with a supply of iced fresh catfish, corn meal coating, onions, batter and cole slaw. Besides Jr. Miller the crew included Mary Ellen Miller, Mike Miller, Suilon Benjamin and Bernice "Bernie" Krolczyk. Arriving at the downtown Athletic Club, the Millers discovered a commercial kitchen with extremely outdated equipment, including gas-fired deep fryers. Though Maurice Corya had projected only 60 dinners for the night, the crew prepared nearly 125 pounds of catfish. To be on the safe side, the Millers had iced and loaded nearly 300 pounds on the van. Mike Miller recollects why the extra fish were loaded, "We had the extra room so we took them down there. We just always hated the thought of not being prepared." After going through a quick review of the menu with the wait staff, dinner orders started coming in and within minutes a deluge of orders flooded the kitchen. According to Mike Miller, "We couldn't believe how many people showed up. We were having trouble preparing the fish with inadequate gas fryers. We couldn't get the grease to recover its temperature fast enough and we had to keep the fish in for an extra minute or so—and back in Colfax that was a strict no-no. To top it off, we found the club staff was eating the food about as fast as we could prepare it. Before the evening was over, we'd served the entire 300 pounds of fish." The Miller's staff ended the night so exhausted they didn't have the energy to eat the sandwiches the regular kitchen staff had prepared; their fatigue was exacerbated by the feeling they had not sent a "Miller's quality" meal into the club's dining room.

Upon his return to Colfax, Jr. Miller sent an invoice to Maurice Corya for the evening's service. It was accompanied by a letter profusely apologizing for the sub-standard meal and, by Miller's standards, poor service. He closed the letter by telling Corya, "We've discovered it's best to play in our own backyard. I doubt if we ever do something like that again." The quality of the food proved to be far better than Jr. Miller and his staff had thought. Within two weeks, a steady flow of dinner patrons from the Athletic Club appeared at the restaurant in Colfax seeking a reprise to their Thanksgiving week dining experience. The Millers were pleased they had another opportunity to show the Athletic Club diners what a real Miller's fish supper tasted like. Mike Miller said the night made the family's mind up. "We didn't care if people thought it went well, we just decided it was best for us to try to become well known in a small town than to try and make it in a big city; the big city just wasn't our style."

By the late '60s, Jr. Miller had begun to ponder the future of his business. Having enjoyed success that had exceeded even his most optimistic expectations, he pledged he would retire by the time he reached age 55. He avowed he would not follow the path of both his parents who had died shortly after their 56th birthday not having ever traveled out of Clinton County. "I was determined I was going to see the world while I was still young enough to do it."

Jr. Miller had also lived his professional life with an emotional burden that had been created by his parents. James O. and Anna May Miller had lived their lives as devoutly religious people and both held a vehement opposition to the consumption of alcohol. His parents, members of

Frankfort's United Brethren Church, attended all night prayer vigils in early 1932 when the debate surfaced over the repeal of the 18th amendment that had outlawed liquor sales; the amendment was ratified just 17 days before James L. Miller's birth. After the death of her husband in 1932, Anna May Miller continued to attend meetings where prayers were offered in hope of preventing the return of alcohol by the drink. It was to no avail, the 21st amendment was ratified on December 5, 1933—Indiana had been among the first states to ratify. Anna May Miller's prayers intensified for those who would be tempted by liquor. Yet, ten years after the death of his mother, James L. Miller had become a partner in one of the most notorious beer joints in Clinton County.

In the earliest days of Miller's restaurant and before Jr. had achieved his goal of transforming his tavern into a family restaurant, old acquaintances from his days at Scroggy School would come to Miller's. Some, after surveying the barroom setting, would confront the youngest Miller son with the heart-wrenching question, "What would your parents think about this?" Jr. Miller spent nearly fifty years pondering the question; he had no idea what his parents would have thought of his business venture. Would the love of their son over-ridden their religious beliefs? Would they have disowned him? Had fate put Earl Anderson in his path to provide surrogate opposition to what he was attempting to accomplish? Whatever it might have been, it factored into his decision to not be part of Miller's beyond February 1974.

Most believed it was a given that Mike Miller would assume ownership of the family's business. Yet, upon his graduation from Clinton Prairie High School in 1966, he was not compelled to follow in his father's footsteps. He assumed if his father followed through with his pledge to retire in 1974, the business would be sold. Even though Mike Miller did come into the business in 1970, it began a period where it looked as if outsiders would eventually own Miller's.

Mike Miller grew up in the restaurant business, but not part of it. He went through high school as a classic underachiever, more interested in moving to California to pursue the development of his noteworthy artistic skills in the customized car business. This desire was the ulterior motive in his asking for a paid trip to California when queried about what he wanted as a graduation present. The trip allowed him to research opportunities that might be available for him on the West Coast. He contacted noted custom car designer, Ed "Big Daddy" Roth, and was told there would be an opportunity for him if he pursued formal art training.

Upon his return to Indiana, Mike began to investigate art schools. However, the U.S. government had different, short-term plans for him. Mike Miller received his draft notice in April 1967 at the height of the Vietnam War. He entered the service in June and was assigned to Ft. Sill, Oklahoma for basic training. He became engaged before departing for Ft. Sill, promising his fiancée that they would be married within three months of his return from the service. Aptitude testing led to his assignment to artillery school where, while his math skills were weak, he dedicated himself to staying in the barracks to study while the rest of his outfit went into Lawton to party. He achieved passing marks during his training, but found it difficult to deal with the emotional stress that accompanied the possibility of making an error and the potential disaster that could accompany such a miscalculation. After seeking the advice of a superior, he "tanked" the remaining tests and was eventually transferred from artillery school to the mess hall.

Jr. Miller was able to later affect issues like billboards and parking spaces in the '70s, but he found out in 1967 that there was no stopping a country looking to escalate a war in Southeast Asia—it needed bodies. Though he was asthmatic and completely deaf in one ear, Mike Miller was inducted into the Army. Ralph Ashley made a direct appeal on behalf of his grandson to Senator Vance Hartke, but no intervention took place. The number of troops being sent overseas had escalated dramatically, but Mike assumed that, because of his infirmities, he would be among the troops remaining in the United States during the war—he was wrong; in August 1968 he found himself in the midst of a combat zone where he was assigned to the mess operation at Cam Rahn Bay. He spent an uneventful ten months in Vietnam, experiencing only occasional assaults as he traveled the roads connecting the Bay with other camps. He returned from Vietnam on June 13, 1969.

During his tour in Vietnam, Mike came to the realization that working in California was not a realistic long-term plan. He wrote his father, telling him that upon his return he would like to discuss his becoming part of the family business. His fiancée had begun working at Miller's while Mike was in the service and after arriving back in the States, Mike immediately began working at the restaurant. Details for assuming partial ownership of the business were drawn up; it appeared the business would remain in the Miller family.

With the business still growing, the Millers determined they needed additional cold storage for the increasing shipments of catfish. The property to the west of the main dining room was purchased and a third section of Miller's was constructed, connecting it to the western wall of the old Keyes' pool room that had been purchased in 1952. By 1971, the Wesleyan Church had moved to a new location and the old G.A.R. building had been torn down. This time, the Millers were in no danger of having the expansion shut down by the Alcoholic Beverage Commission. Ironically, the lot where the Wesleyan Church had once played a role in nearly halting the first expansion of Miller's was now owned by the Millers and was being used as a parking lot for their customers. Customer parking was always a concern for the Millers. Colfax was a small town, but they wanted their customers to have the shortest possible walk and to also remain close enough to hear the loudspeaker calling out numbers. Most people would initiate a petition drive to stop a project that included the construction of a parking lot within 15 feet of their home, but not the Millers. When a small house adjacent to Jr. and Mary Ellen Miller's home was put up for sale, they purchased the house, razed it and replaced it with a paved parking lot that covered the entire lot; the new parking area put Miller's customers only a block and a half from a table in the restaurant.

The expansion included significantly larger coolers and kitchen equipment. Since the space was available, the Millers decided it could be transformed into a third dining room and be used for large parties and the overflow crowds on weekend nights. A full-service kitchen was added to the new dining area, including deep fryers and another auger fryer similar to the one that had been installed in the original barroom cooking area. The company that had originally manufactured the auger fryer had gone out of business, but the Millers found a used auger and purchased it for $500; it would turn out to be the most expensive investment they ever made. The business celebrated its 25th anniversary in 1971 and to outsiders Miller's appeared to be continuing to gain momentum. While customer counts were the highest in the business' history, an internal situation was brewing that would threaten the Miller family's magnificent run in Colfax.

Mike Miller married his fiancée in August 1969; however, the marriage quickly ran aground. By his own admission, his marriage was a mistake. He had not played out his desire to run around and his late night escapades

127

with friends were creating intolerable stress in the marriage. By the summer of 1972, the marriage had deteriorated completely, finally crumbling one night when Mike moved out of the couple's house. After spending the night with friends Jim and Jo Ellen Street, Mike got word that his father wanted to speak with him. His wife had called Jr. and Mary Ellen to tell them of the previous night's altercation and Mike's departure. When Mike made an appearance at the restaurant and admitted his intentions to seek a divorce, his father reacted by telling him he was no longer welcome to be part of the family's business.

Jr. Miller had a deep-seated belief in the sanctity of marriage and he felt his son had not made a commitment to making his work. Mike responded with equally irrational emotion, telling his father that if that's what he wanted it was fine with him. He returned to the Street's house to ponder what he should do. He and the Streets set out for Atlanta, Georgia where a Frankfort acquaintance lived. The friend in Atlanta had connections in the construction business and Mike had decided he'd pursue a job as far from Colfax as he could possibly get. Waitresses remember that they avoided any direct contact with Jr. Miller during the days immediately following the confrontation with his son. Mike Miller's departure had been the first time his father had seemed to lose control of a situation and the elder Miller was not handling it well.

Mike Miller returned a few days later to take care of some personal business, including filing official documents relating to his divorce. During his stay he once again received word that his father wanted to talk with him. He was reluctant to see his father and receive, what he assumed, would be another lecture about his failings as a husband, but decided to see his father before returning to Georgia; he had no idea when he might return to his hometown or, if he would ever return again. By the time of the second meeting the two men had gotten their emotions under control and father and son talked for several hours. Jr. Miller asked his son to return to Colfax and resume his entry into the business, albeit on a probationary basis. Mike agreed to return, making it clear he still intended to follow through with the divorce from his wife.

During the summer of 1972, an attractive young lady applied for a job at Miller's. Beckie Dieterle had recently graduated from Ball State University with a degree in elementary education and saw the job at Miller's as a way to generate income while she looked for a full time teaching position. The lovely brunette's energy and effusive personality immediately began to earn her a following of regular customers; Mike's soon-to-be ex-wife continued to work at Miller's as well. Mike's divorce became final in August 1973 and his ex-wife departed the business. In the meantime, Beckie Dieterle had decided to remain employed at Miller's; she had begun to earn nearly twice as much as a starting teacher's salary (most school corporations were offering beginning teachers annual salaries of $6,000 or less) during a time when tip income wasn't always fully reported. She also had not escaped the eye of the man who was now in the process of assuming management of his family's business. Mike Miller gazed from the barroom through the window into the main dining room one night and realized he was looking at the woman who could bring stability to his life. He turned to friend Jim Street, who was seated at the bar, and vowed that he was certain he would someday ask the charming might-have-been schoolteacher to marry him. Mike Miller and Rebecca Rae Dieterle were married on January 6, 1974, less than a month before the February 2nd date Jr. Miller had declared would be his last in the restaurant business. Mike Miller's second marriage did bring stability to his life and to his family's business. The stability ensured that Miller's would remain in the Miller family for another twenty years and allowed Jr. and Mary Ellen Miller to embark on following through with Jr.'s goal of seeing the world. The only incongruity of Mike Miller's assumption of the management of his family's business was that he is allergic to fish. He learned to prepare catfish as well as his father ever could, he just couldn't eat them.

Mike and Beckie Miller made a seamless transition from Jr. and Mary Ellen Miller's management of the business. Miller's enjoyed its highest volume years during Mike Miller's first several years of management. Staff members saw no difference in the operation with Mike in charge. Connie Pritchard confirms the ease of transition, "Mike and Beckie were just like Jr. and Mary Ellen. They were strict, but fun to work with because they cared so much for their people. Mike had the same rules as his dad but just like with Jr., even though you had to work hard, he made sure there was time to play." The dedication of the staff was tested in 1980.

Though it was mid-January, the weather of January 19, 1980 was clear and the new room was open in anticipation of a large Saturday night crowd. Fryers, including the auger fryer, which held 20 pounds more grease than the fryers used for catfish, were turned on and were waiting for the first batch of catfish and onion rings. The doors opened at precisely 4:00 p.m. and approximately 30 customers who had been conditioned to arrive early in order to avoid a lengthy wait filed through the doors. The thirty were seated among the tables in the small dining room adjacent to the bar and in what had become known since 1971 as the main dining room.

After opening the doors to the restaurant, Beckie Miller walked to the new dining room area to make one last inspection of its readiness. As she pushed open the glass door separating the new room from the main dining area she saw Bernie Krolczyk leap over the counter that separated the fryers from the dining area. Krolczyk let out a loud yell as she landed on her feet alerting anyone within earshot that one of the fryers had caught fire.

Mike and Beckie Miller, 1975

Beckie Miller turned back into the main dining room and shouted for the waitresses to evacuate the dining areas and alert Mike to the situation. He arrived within seconds and immediately went to a wall-mounted fire extinguisher. By the time he'd reached the extinguisher, flames had begun to leap up four feet from the fryer. He then activated a powdered flame retardant system only to discover that the spouts containing the powdery substance had been positioned to expel their contents directly into the fryers—the flames that had climbed up the back wall were unaffected by the system. The hand-held fire extinguisher had no effect on slowing the spread of the fire, which had now moved into the other fryers and ignited anything flammable behind the counter.

The only decision that could be made was to go back into the main section of the restaurant to ensure that everyone had been evacuated from the building. Mary Rominger, who worked at the restaurant from 1976 through 1989 and was on duty when the fire ignited, provided testimony to some customer's obsession with Miller's food. "We got everyone to leave but one man. He told me he wasn't leaving until he got his onion rings. I finally had to tell him that if he stayed any longer he was going to end up looking like one of our onion rings. He wasn't happy about it, but he did finally leave." After checking both restrooms, Mike Miller turned to exit the building, turning once to look into the new dining room as the flames roared behind the glass door; he wasn't sure if any of the building would be left standing.

The Colfax Volunteer Fire Department quickly responded, having called the nearby Clarks Hill Fire Department for assistance. The Frankfort Fire Department was called and its special foam unit was immediately dispatched to Colfax. Although the fire department arrived within minutes, the fire was raging out of control. Fireman called in a backhoe operator to knock a hole in the sidewall to gain access to the restaurant, but it proved to be too late to save any of the contents of the newest part of the facility. It was nearly 7:00 p.m. before the fire was completely extinguished.

Daybreak on January 20 revealed the grim reality of the fire; it had devastated the newest section of the restaurant, while the balance of the restaurant was heavily damaged by smoke and water. Anyone observing the burned-out building might have concluded that January 19, 1980 would be marked as the end of Miller's; anyone but Jr. and Mike Miller. When interviewed by a number of central Indiana newspapers that had come to Colfax to cover the aftermath of the fire, both were adamant in their resolve—Miller's would reopen and it would reopen soon.

The co-owners laid out a reconstruction plan that would allow them to follow through with their promise. The ordeal that followed was particularly traumatic for Beckie Miller. She had become pregnant in early January and, only 22 days after the fire, the Miller family lost the man who had played an immeasurably important role in building their business; Ralph Ashley died on February 10, 1980. Because Mike and Beckie were unsure of her pregnancy, they had chosen to not inform Ralph and Irene Ashley until they were certain. Ralph Ashley died not knowing about his grandchild, Louis Thomas Miller, who was born October 17, 1980.

It was decided the damage in the new section of the restaurant would be ignored in the early going. The focus of the reconstruction plan was to be on the older two sections where only smoke and water damage had occurred. The Miller's brought in local contractor, and close friend, George Benefiel to supervise the clean up and reconstruction of the business. Benefiel, owner of Benny's Construction, had a crew of his own, but he also found a number of the Miller's staff eager to help any way they could. Nancy Dowell was one of the people who made the trip to Colfax every day.

133

"Of course we wanted the restaurant to open up as soon as possible—we wanted to go back to work. But a lot of us could have gotten jobs somewhere else. The real reason so many of us wanted to help was that none of us wanted to work anywhere else but Miller's. The Millers were part of our family and you stand by your family when they need help."

While the repairs afforded an opportunity to do some remodeling, very little was changed. Jr. Miller told people around Colfax, "We want to pretty much put it back the way it was. We don't want to doll it up too much." The only significant change in the original dining room saw the red-flocked wallpaper replaced with a more conservative design—the rest of the decor was replicated. Benefiel and his crew, including the Miller's employees, began working to restore Miller's, often working eighteen to twenty hour days. It was not Benefiel's first experience with reconstructing the Miller's business. According to Mike Miller, "George had saved us on several occasions dating back to the break-ins. When thieves broke out the large windows George dropped everything to repair the place. We probably couldn't have stayed open without him. He's just been an important part of our business for a long time."

The cause of the fire was initially attributed to faulty wiring. The Millers knew their building was aging rapidly; their concern with the electrical system had prompted them to completely rewire the older sections of the business in 1979. They had not concerned themselves with the newer section that had been built in 1971. It was eventually determined that the auger fryer had been the source of the blaze. Purchased used when the new room was built, the thermostat on the fryer had malfunctioned and allowed grease to heat to the point of ignition; the $500 piece of equipment had been responsible for causing over $200,000 in damage.

Aftermath of January 19, 1980 fire.

The 1980 Miller's fire had been extinguished at 7:00 p.m. on January 19. At 4:00 p.m. on March 5, 1980 the doors to the original two sections of the restaurant were unlocked for customers. Only 44 days had elapsed from the moment when many questioned whether Miller's would ever reopen to the moment when the first batch of fish was pulled from the fryers in the bar area kitchen. Benefiel then went to work renovating the new section and it reopened in mid-May 1980—only four months after being completely destroyed.

The early damage estimates proved to be accurate. By the time the new room had reopened, repair costs totaled slightly more than $200,000. Over $40,000 of the repair costs came out-of-pocket after proceeds from the $160,000 insurance policy had been depleted. The rebirth of Miller's had been a tribute to a group of dedicated employees, George Benefiel and, several local suppliers who were willing to drop everything else they were doing to ensure that the Colfax landmark would continue on.

Chapter Eight

"It was just time to go."

The honk from a passing car shattered Jr. Miller's trance as he had fixed his eyes on the canopied, stucco covered building across the street; he was unsure how much time had passed while he stood at the corner. He was finding it difficult to cross the street on this, his last night as owner of Miller's Restaurant. Mike Miller had arrived earlier than usual and had prepared the fryers for the last night when his father walked into the dining room area behind the bar. The two men engaged in idle conversation, avoiding any mention of the significance of the night to come. For those who have never dedicated their life to a business of their own, it may be difficult to understand the distress attached to contemplating a life without that business, yet in the winter of 1993, Jr. and Mike Miller began a series of discussions that confronted the possibility of life without the restaurant.

When queried about the decision to sell their business, both Jr. and Mike Miller would only respond, "It was just time to go." However an examination of the Miller's daily business records chronicles a significant change in customer counts from 1970 to the early 1990s. During the period 1970 to 1976, Miller's experienced the highest annual customer counts in its history, with 1976 being the highest count ever when over 135,000 customers passed through its doors. The substantial increase in business from 1973 to 1976 proved the skeptics who had predicted that Miller's would suffer in the transition of management from Jr. Miller to his son to be wrong. The next several years proved that Mike and Beckie Miller would maintain the same business philosophy as the founders of the business. Velera Cain confirms that there was little difference when the second generation took the reins, "They were just like Jr. and Mary Ellen, they were there all the time. Beckie worked just as hard as Mary Ellen ever did. When it boils down to it, I think that's what people liked as much as the food—they could come someplace where they knew the same people were going to be there to take care of them every time, especially when those people included the owners."

The atrocious winter of 1977 brought a fifteen percent decrease in business, with the months of January and February contributing 95% of the decrease in the year's customer count. The restaurant was closed for fourteen business days, and even when they attempted to open during inclement weather, there were two nights when a total of two pounds of fish were served each night during business hours. Attempting to open no matter how harsh the weather was typical for the Millers; they never wanted to disappoint any customer who had made the effort to come to their restaurant no matter how inclement the weather might be. The winter of 1978 was no kinder and the business experienced another five percent decline in business. The numbers from 1977 and 1978 never recovered upward to the peak year of 1976. However, the business stabilized at the 1978 level and remained steady for ten years, with annual customer counts exceeding the 100,000 mark through 1987. The restaurant had begun to be cited in a number of "Best of" awards from various sources. *Indianapolis Monthly* readers had named Miller's "Best Place for Catfish" in a 1985 poll and two years later, it was named "Best Country Diner" in the same poll. The restaurant invariably was named the best place for catfish and onion rings in the Lafayette *Journal and Courier*'s circulation area. In Mike Miller's opinion, the most important "Best of" cited in the *Journal and Courier* polls was that his business had been named as a place for the best service.

Miller's also received significant regional attention. The premier issue of Meredith Publishing's *Midwest Living* was launched in April 1987. Of the hundreds of restaurants in the Midwest that might have been chosen for its restaurant review feature, the publication selected Miller's to be among the three included in the premier issue. The review included a photograph of Mike and Beckie Miller and Velera Cain. Tom Warren of the Corvallis, Oregon *Gazette-Times* had visited Miller's ten years before. He had been so impressed with the restaurant that he returned to Corvallis to run a full-page photo essay proclaiming to his readers he had discovered "Catfish-Town USA" in a little town called Colfax.

Other than 1980 when the fire forced a forty-four day closing, the years between 1979 and 1987 saw no more than a two percent fluctuation in customer counts, again mostly depending upon the vagaries of the Indiana winter. After a steady ten year run, the business suffered an eight percent decrease in both 1988 and 1989, but 1992 was to be the year that began to determine the fate of Miller's. When the year's business was tallied, the numbers showed that Miller's had done exactly fifty percent of its peak year of 1976. Another small decrease in 1993 pointed to the reality that Miller's was in danger of losing money for the first time ever; the decision to put the business on the market was made in early January 1994. Another issue that had begun to create pressure on Mike and Beckie Miller was staffing. While experienced waitresses like Velera Cain, Connie Pritchard, Nancy Dowell, and Suilon Benjamin remained on the staff, additional waitresses were needed on weekends and by the early '90s they were becoming difficult to locate—especially ones who could work under the pressure of a Miller's weekend night. An examination of employment records during the period 1991 to 1994 exposed an alarming number of waitresses who worked less than three weeks for Miller's; most new hires had never experienced the kind of work demands they found in Colfax and simply chose to quit.

There may be a number of reasons why the business began to decline. As it entered the late '80s, Miller's was faced with a dining public that, for the most part, had now become addicted to fast food and, in turn, was beginning to accept lower quality food standards in favor of convenience. Another issue facing Miller's was the age of its core customer group. One magazine reviewer pointed to the nostalgic '50s feel of the restaurant—a look that proved comfortable for Miller's older clientele, but made it appear stodgy and outdated to younger customers. The sons and daughters of older customers had continued to embrace Miller's, but even that generation was becoming older themselves and their children were now completely oriented to fast food.

For most restaurants located fifty miles from the state capitol, the growing restaurant population in Marion County would not have been a concern. However, the Millers understood how important the market area was for them. In 1963 when state license plates began to identify the county of origin, Jr. Miller would send his son and a friend out to wander a five-block radius of the restaurant. Their task was to write down the county of every car parked along Colfax's streets; the teenage boys conducting the research were hard pressed to explain the presence of a car carrying plates from Hawaii. It was an unscientific market research process, but it gave Jr. Miller the information he wanted; by the late 1960's over forty percent of his business was coming from Marion, Hamilton and Hendricks counties. Another twenty percent were traveling over thirty miles from counties north of Lafayette. It was gratifying that people were traveling long distances to eat at Miller's, but as the metropolitan area of Indianapolis began to grow, dozens of alternatives to Miller's were being opened each year; by 1990 the Marion County business began to noticeably decline.

Fast food was taking the hardest toll on weekday numbers. Fast food restaurants were not allowed membership in the Indiana Restaurant Association, now called the Restaurant & Hospitality Association of Indiana, in the '50s and '60s, but once admitted, over 350 were listed in the 1995 association directory, with many single memberships representing multiple store ownership. While people were still willing to travel to Colfax on weekend nights, the convenience of the proliferation of hamburger, pizza and fried chicken joints made it too easy to make a ten minute round trip from home on Tuesdays, Wednesdays and Thursdays. Weekend numbers, for the most part, held steady, but by 1991 weekday customer counts had plummeted.

The '90s also saw a significant increase in the number of restaurants that included catfish on their menus. While many people admit most could not measure up to Miller's, convenience again prompted a growing number of the dining public to make the compromise. Some felt the Miller's menu had fallen from grace due to a growing nationwide emphasis on healthier food; deep fried catfish and onion rings were never found on any list of health foods. The focus on healthier eating probably had little to do with Miller's declining numbers; consumption of fat-laden double and triple hamburgers at fast food chains continued to significantly increase.

In the end, it most likely wasn't a health issue, but one of convenience. People, particularly younger customers, didn't want to wait for a meal. To a generation who didn't possess the patience to wait for water to boil, there was little romance in waiting an hour for a table and by the early 1990s the proliferation of corporate restaurants who served meals in the $10-12 range had offered so many options that people didn't have to wait. They knew that if the Outback® was busy that they could get essentially the same meal at the Lone Star® Steakhouse or any one of the look-alikes; the same held true for Applebee's® and its many clones. The draw of Miller's unique menu and atmosphere was no longer an attraction, but a detriment. The Millers still held out hope that after people tried out the new places they would return to Colfax. What they hadn't calculated was the flood of new restaurants would not ebb. Heading into the 21st century Indiana has 25% more chain restaurants than the national average and Indianapolis has an even greater percentage than the national norm with nearly 60% of its restaurants being part of chains.

Another issue with Miller's declining customer counts was its profit margins. People were aware of the huge volume of business Miller's enjoyed in its peak years. However, the Miller's profit margin philosophy precluded it from being the lucrative cash cow most people assumed it to be. Jr. Miller was quoted in a Lafayette *Journal and Courier* article, "Heck, I'm not greedy. I don't want to make a lot of money. All I want to do is make a decent living." His income goal drove the Miller's pricing policy. From the day they bought the business, the Millers found it excruciating to raise menu prices, sometimes experiencing two or three food price increases before they would reflect them in their retail pricing. Even then, the price increases accounted only for the wholesale price changes without factoring in any additional margin percentage on the increases. The Miller's margin strategy was based on volume and customer counts had to remain high; the cost of doing business had risen significantly over the years. The annual payroll of $8,300 in 1946 had grown to nearly $160,000 in 1976. Most other expenses were rising at a quicker pace than the Miller's reluctant response in reflecting the increases in their menu prices. The Millers remained cautious about making any significant changes to their pricing policy, believing that the changes would reduce customer counts further.

The Millers initially listed the business for sale through the Restaurant & Hospitality Association of Indiana; nearly a year passed without an inquiry. Cheri Cooper of Metropolitan Real Estate in Lafayette had learned that the Millers were seeking a buyer and contacted Jr. Miller in January 1995. Yet, when she talked to him she was told the business was not for sale. During the days following Cheri Cooper's call, Jr. Miller pondered what he had told her. "I had asked the Lord for guidance and realized that He was providing me an opportunity. I had to follow through with what He was giving me." Jr. Miller called Cheri Cooper and entered into an agreement for her to pursue possible buyers. The Millers provided extensive business records to Cooper and she counseled them on what a reasonable asking price should be. The potential buyers that first came into play discovered they were not in a position to acquire the necessary funding to purchase the business. Finally, Cooper presented a buyer who was in a position to make the purchase if the Miller's would consider selling their business on contract. The potential buyer was Dan Furry.

Dan Furry was owner/manager of Furry, Inc., a machine shop in Danville, Illinois that had been founded by his father in 1955. Furry was no stranger to the restaurant business. He had purchased Stiney's in 1985, a well-known restaurant operation first opened by Pauline and "Stiney" Stinebaugh in 1957. Located on the South River Road outside of West Lafayette, Indiana, Stiney's was one of several restaurants opened in the '50s that featured fried catfish on its menu. Whether it was an attempt to mimic Miller's success (the long lines at Miller's had begun to form in 1948), or simply a coincidence, few people felt Stiney's, or any of the other imitators could match Miller's. Bob Higman was one who felt the other catfish restaurants never measured up. "We'd go to Pittsboro once in a while. It was good—but it just wasn't Miller's. They were one of a kind."

143

A number of reviewers agreed with Higman. John Schroeder, writing in the Winter/Spring, '85-86 edition of the Purdue University edition of *National Campus* magazine chose Miller's to review because "it is an institution where the name is synonymous with catfish."

After reviewing Miller's business records, Metropolitan Real Estate presented a purchase offer on Dan Furry's behalf; he offered to purchase Miller's Restaurant for $395,000. The offer was predicated on property and equipment being valued at $199,000 with the goodwill and reputation of Miller's that had been established making up the remaining $196,000 of the purchase price.

Jr. and Mike Miller were astonished by the offer, which was tendered based on a down payment and a contract that called for annual payments spanning nine years. It became clear to the Millers that if the value of the business was over $400,000 after the existing inventory was factored in, it was likely that an outright purchase of the restaurant would prove difficult for most potential buyers. They agreed to underwrite the sale of the business to Dan Furry and the agreement was drawn up. Jr. Miller had high hopes about the future of Miller's. "I thought Dan would be a suitable person to keep the place up. We weren't going to sell the business to just anyone. You've got to remember that our name was still going to be on the front door and I wanted the new owner to live up to our standards." A critical detail in the terms of the sale would become an issue four years later: The Miller's name could only be used as long as Dan Furry owned it. If he elected to ever sell the business, ownership of the Miller's name would revert back to the Miller family. The deal was to be closed on April 17, 1995.

Prior to closing the purchase, Dan Furry had Shirley Haeberle spend two weeks in the restaurant to familiarize herself with the Miller's operation.

Haeberle was an experienced restaurant manager, having managed Stiney's for 24 years. Furry decided that she would continue to manage Stiney's during the day and then travel the thirty miles in time for the 4:00 p.m. opening at Miller's. Mary Ellen and Beckie Miller sensed trouble during the first few days of Haeberle's orientation. The good-natured Haeberle appeared to want nothing to do with the hands-on work that the Miller's had invested to build their business. She declined to work alongside the waitresses to bus tables, distribute numbers to waiting customers, take food orders, or any of the other nuts-and-bolts activities that Mary Ellen and Beckie Miller had been so willing to do. Haeberle saw her role in the business to be more of a public relations position, only willing to wander around the restaurant visiting with customers. She had not shown any inclination to be involved in the business up to the last night of the Miller family's ownership.

To most customers, the evening of April 15, 1995 appeared to be like a typical Saturday night. However, Mike Miller had alerted his friends that it was to be the last night for his family's ownership of the restaurant and most were not going to let such a significant event pass without their participation—they knew that April 15 was not going to be a typical Saturday night at Miller's. They would come to have a good time but also hoping they wouldn't spend the majority of the evening in tears.

A large group of Miller family friends arrived at 6:00 p.m. and were seated at a table that had been expressly reserved for them. It was noteworthy in that it was the first reservation ever accepted by the Miller family. Dwight Slipher, a close friend of the Miller family, had begun to videotape the events of the final evening, when Beckie Miller stopped by the table to inform the group that Slipher wasn't the only cameraman on the premises. She pointed out the dining room window to a man standing outside the restaurant assembling a video camera and tripod from a truck identifying it as being from Channel 13 in Indianapolis. The television station had been alerted to the significance of the evening at Miller's by Dave Feltner, whose wife, Ellen, was a Miller's waitress. The station made the decision to send a film crew to Colfax to cover the Miller family's last night. The feature, which ran on that night's eleven o'clock news, was reported by Kevin Bradley and Linda Ellzroth and included a series of customer interviews.

While the lengthy feature captured Miller's on what appeared to be a typical Saturday night, the camera also captured eyes that showed a deep sadness in the hustle and bustle. The eyes belonged to Mary Ellen Miller as she stood near the door to the old, rickety stairs leading to the dungeon-like basement of Miller's. While she had not said much about the final night, the expression on her face showed she was affected by the reality of the moment. The feature captured Miller's at its best—the title of the feature nearly terminated the sale of the business.

On Monday morning, April 17, 1995, Cheri Cooper and the Miller family were waiting for Dan Furry to arrive at the Metropolitan Real Estate office in Lafayette. Furry burst through the door, livid over the Channel 13 feature and threatening to terminate the purchase agreement. He felt the feature, titled "End of an Era", had positioned the restaurant as closing and would prove to be detrimental to the future of the business. After several minutes of cajoling, Furry regained his composure and proceeded with the closing of the sale. In the end, the title of the Channel 13 feature proved to be prophetic—it was the end of an era—it took fewer than five years for it to end completely.

Miller's Restaurant opened on Tuesday, April 18, 1995 under new ownership and Shirley Haeberle's management; management that was to be short-lived. While she spent two weeks in the restaurant prior to the transfer of ownership, Shirley Haeberle had neglected to learn one tricky thing about the facility. The entrance between the original dining room and the main room ramped up at about a 20-degree incline. One evening during her first week at Miller's as manager, she walked from the main room, slipped and crashed flat on her back. Unlike Bernice Morrow who had jumped to her feet and continued on several years before, Haeberle was seriously injured. Dan Furry was immediately faced with having to put the management of his new business venture in the hands of someone else.

It's not unusual for most businesses to have certain employees who believe they could manage the business better than the owners or managers; Miller's was a case in point. After Shirley Haeberle's accident incapacitated her to a point where she was unable to manage the day-to-day operation, Dan Furry put the business in the hands of Jack Kauffman. Kaufmann, his wife Barbara, and the majority of their children had been employed by Miller's for several years. Later, even though Haeberle had recuperated to a point where she could have returned to Miller's, Kauffman convinced Furry that he was capable of managing the business. Furry agreed and allowed Haeberle to return to Stiney's full time.

Jack Kauffman had been with the Millers for over thirty years and was capable of handling the basics of the nightly operation, including frying fish when called upon. While he had always proved to be a dependable employee, he possessed none of the interpersonal skills necessary to sustain the friendly atmosphere that had been such an integral part of the business' success. He quickly discovered there was much more to the management of a business than turning on the fryers and other basic food preparation. Employee management, customer satisfaction, and inventory management were all very new to Kauffman and he struggled to deal with them all.

Kauffman and his wife also had alienated the majority of the staff when they were supporters of Furry's policy to ban any of the Miller family from the restaurant after the completion of the sale. If any of the Miller family entered the restaurant, employees were instructed to ask them to leave. If they encountered any resistance, employees were to then call the town marshal and have the Millers escorted from the building.

Although she, like her husband, had been a dependable employee, Barbara Kauffman, according to many of the staff, was one of the most vocal in voicing her opinion that she and her husband could manage the business as well, or better, than the Millers, especially Mike and Beckie Miller. Most staff felt that Jack Kauffman had not wanted to assume the responsibilities of managing Miller's, but was convinced by his wife to accept them. Time proved that the management of Miller's wasn't as easy as the Miller family had made it appear.

Eventually, Furry brought in another Kauffman family member to manage the business. Dan Kauffman entered the picture and immediately began making drastic changes in the restaurant's operation and decor. Competitive pressures were dictating that the new management embrace the Miller's principles of operation more than ever; but Dan Kauffman had not calculated that his changes would transform Miller's into "just another restaurant". Miller's was recognized for the last time in October 1995 when it was named the fifth best restaurant in Indiana in *Indiana's Favorite Hometown Restaurants: Where the Local Folks Like To Eat*, a book published by the Indiana Association of Cities and Towns. The poll to establish the contents of the book had been taken during the time when the business was still owned by the Miller family; no accolades would ever follow. Under new management the Miller's mystique dissipated at an alarming pace.

The changes that most disturbed the staff who had worked under the Miller family's management came in both food quality and cleanliness. Business was deteriorating because of an attitude by Jack Kauffman that if a customer was dissatisfied they should go someplace else and many were doing just that. The rapid decline in numbers was also dictating that corners be cut in food quality. The most significant change in food quality was a violation of Jr. Miller's inviolate "clean grease" policy. Dan Furry had told the Lafayette *Journal and Courier* during an interview shortly after his purchase of the restaurant that, "I won't change the product or the process," but he and his manager decided the cost of the special grease-cleansing filters was not a justifiable expense; the special filters were replaced with cheesecloth. Filtering grease through cheese cloth created the illusion that it was being readied for another day's use, but in reality, it removed none of the contaminates the special filters had been designed to remove; a critical Miller's process had been severely compromised. It wasn't long before waitresses were hearing comments that the catfish "just didn't taste the same."

Customers were also noticing a change in the cleanliness of the restaurant; a condition staff members confirm was becoming distressing. The most graphic example of the deterioration of the restaurant's condition came from a service technician employed by the Tri-County Telephone Company. The repairman had often frequented Miller's as a customer and one day was called to repair a telephone in the restaurant. It had been reported that the telephone in the bar was malfunctioning; while a caller could call out on the telephone, incoming calls were not producing any perceptible ringing in the phone.

When the repairman arrived, he unplugged the telephone and returned to his truck to inspect it. Upon removing the telephone's cover, the repairman was startled to discover why the apparatus had not been producing a ringing sound. A mountain of deceased cockroaches tumbled from the phone when its cover had been removed. The density of the tiny corpses was so great it had finally muffled the bell apparatus in the phone. The repairman removed the remaining dead insects, replaced the cover and returned the phone to the restaurant's bar. He, on the other hand, chose to never frequent Miller's again.

By the first of July 1999 Dan Furry decided he'd had enough of the restaurant business. Citing a need to devote his full-time attention to his Danville machine shop, he announced on July 7th that Miller's would close on July 24, 1999. The restaurant was put up for sale the week of the announcement it would close. Cheri Cooper's company again found itself attempting to sell the business she'd brokered just four years before; Metropolitan Real Estate had earlier brokered the sale of Stiney's for Furry the previous March. Unlike Miller's, Stiney's was still operating at the time of its sale but, like Miller's, a decline in food quality and service under Furry's ownership had drastically reduced customer counts. Some had started referring to the restaurant as "Stinkey's" because of the overall condition of the business. Todd and Jo Ann McGraw purchased Stiney's and, after giving the business a thorough cleaning, initially attempted to operate the restaurant under the franchise name. The stigma that had engulfed the property during Furry's ownership proved too much to overcome. In the early going, the McGraw's retained Shirley Haeberle; however her stay was short-lived. According to Todd McGraw, "It became obvious she wasn't willing to work at the pace we knew it would take for us to be successful," confirming Beckie and Mary Ellen Miller's earlier suspicion about Haeberle's reluctance to commit to the rudimentary, but critical, tasks of the restaurant business. In August 1999 the McGraws implemented a plan to reinvent their riverside establishment. Closing the restaurant in early August, the couple invested over $250,000 in a major renovation of the property and implemented a significant makeover of their menu. Reopening in February 2000 as McGraw's, the newly invented restaurant quickly gained favor among area diners and has become known for its weekend crowds.

Most restaurants quietly come and go, but the news of Miller's warranted major coverage in several Indiana newspapers; the publicity also generated renewed interest in the restaurant from around the state of Indiana. Derrick Gingery reported in *The Times* of Frankfort that Dan Furry was reconsidering his decision to close Miller's. Furry was quoted as saying he would review the numbers over the coming weeks and make a decision about the future of the restaurant. His comments still had the tone of a man who would most likely not reverse his decision to sell a business that, even though he claimed he needed to reallocate his time to his machine shop, was failing. A group of Colfax residents was not relying on Furry to change his mind. Several people were contacted in an attempt to pursue the possibility of purchasing Miller's as a cooperative.

Derrick Gingery reported on July 23, 1999 that Dan Furry had changed his mind. News of the closing had generated a new wave of business that had moved Furry to keep Miller's open past the original July 24 closing date. Though Furry decided to not close Miller's, he remained openly skeptical that the increased numbers could be sustained; Cheri Cooper continued to search for a potential buyer. Furry may have exposed his true motivation for selling Miller's in a quote in Gingery's report, "As long as they (the employees) are willing to try, I can work through this. I would like to get it sold and see if someone else can make it work." The prospect of a group of investors purchasing the business had run into legal problems, making it appear unlikely that the option for saving Miller's would be possible; Miller's would survive only 25 more days.

It became clear that the spike up in business during the days following the announcement the restaurant would close was driven by nostalgia; people just had to have one last look at Miller's before it closed, regardless of how badly the quality of the operation had deteriorated. The doors of one of the most famous restaurants in Indiana history were locked for the last time on August 17, 1999. Probably because of the many false alarms about Miller's closing, the final day of the business went unmentioned by the Frankfort newspaper. Dan Furry had endured the predictable fate of a disinterested, absentee owner. He had bought two "name brand" restaurants apparently assuming the brand names would have adequate inertia to sustain each business at acceptable revenue levels. In the end, his apathy toward each business led to their demise. Stiney's was reclaimed under a new name and is being operated with a classic Miller's-style management philosophy by Todd and Jo Ann McGraw; Miller's was not to be as fortunate.

Metropolitan Real Estate intensified its search for a buyer with the financial resources to buy Miller's, but found they were contending with two significant obstacles in its path. The first was money; Furry had established an asking price of $350,000. While the price was $45,000 less than Furry had paid just over four years before, it's assumed that annual revenue had significantly deteriorated from the business' last year under the Miller family when it had suffered the first net loss in its history. The second, and most critical issue was the stipulation that the sale of the business would not include the Miller's name. Dan Furry was attempting to sell a franchise without its defining identity. Few were interested in buying Miller's if it couldn't be operated as Miller's. Those who did express interest, and appeared unconcerned that their purchase would not include the

Miller's name, most often did not have the resources to make the significant financial investment to purchase the business.

The fall of 2000 approached without any legitimate prospect; Miller's sat, frozen in time. The windows of the building had been boarded over, but when a sheet of plywood came loose from a side window, it was revealed that the interior of the restaurant appeared to be out of a scene from a science fiction movie. Miller's had been closed over a year, yet the interior of the restaurant looked as though it was ready to open. Tables were set with dust-covered plates, silverware, glasses, and napkins. The scene would lead a person to assume that the business was simply abandoned after August 17, 1999; someone had turned off the lights and simply walked away. Residents of Colfax were accepting the inevitable; if Miller's hadn't sold by now, it was highly unlikely it would ever sell. Speculation began to swirl about Furry's plan for the property. Many had hoped he'd be willing to accept a loss and reduce the selling price of the business to a point where someone could purchase it. On the afternoon of December 13, 2000 the selling price of Miller's became a moot point.

The Colfax Fire Department received a call at 12:58 p.m. reporting smoke coming from the Miller's building. By the time firefighters arrived in the midst of a heavy snowfall, the building was in flames. Hampered by the depletion of the town water supply, the collapse of an interior stairway that prevented access to the 2nd floor where Jr. and Mary Ellen had first made their home, and the snow that had accumulated on the streets, firefighters could do very little to extinguish the fire. Flames were still rolling up from the second floor at 8:00 p.m. and were finally extinguished an hour later. When daybreak came the following day, the people of Colfax knew that, unlike the January, 1980 fire, this time there would be no resurrection of their most famous landmark.

It took less than 24 hours for investigators to determine that the fire that had destroyed 50 years of the Miller family's life memories had been intentionally set. Evidence clearly pointed to the fire igniting in the stairway leading to the second floor. Nothing in the stairway could have possibly ignited accidentally; some sort of incendiary device had been placed along the old wooden steps leading to the upstairs storage areas. The arson ruling set off a storm of speculation about who had set the fire; the situation surrounding the previous 16 months prompted many to make unfounded assumptions about who might be responsible. At the time the fire was first reported, Dan Furry was aboard a commercial jet on his way to North Carolina. By the summer of 2002 arson investigators had made no progress in identifying the arsonist; it's doubtful the identity will ever be known. While insurance payments have been withheld during the investigation, Dan Furry has continued to follow through with his contract obligations to the Millers; two installments have been made since the fire and the Millers have no reason to believe that Furry will renege on subsequent payments.

There is a larger issue than whether the payment schedule from a sales contract will be fulfilled. The center of the little Indiana farm town is irreparably scarred. The burned-out shell of the building that once housed Bert John's hotel, Brooks' Restaurant, and then, one of the most famous restaurants in Indiana business history has created an atmosphere of depression in the community. The crowded streets of a Saturday night have dissipated to a handful of locals who loiter across the street from Miller's in front of Colfax's only tavern. Most newspaper articles written about Colfax since the Miller's fire have primarily been to chronicle the political infighting between the town council and its contentious town clerk. People in Colfax know that with each passing year, fewer people will remember Colfax and the notoriety it once enjoyed. Yet, there are many towns that never enjoyed the celebrity that Miller's brought to Colfax. The town's appearance hasn't changed much over the years. Driving around Colfax, one discovers it to be a collection of well-kept homes sitting among some that appear to be within days of collapsing. However, if the appearance of Colfax hasn't changed, the feel of the town seems to have changed significantly.

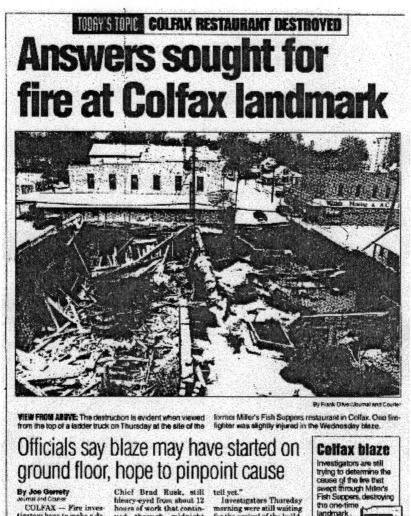

TODAY'S TOPIC **COLFAX RESTAURANT DESTROYED**

Answers sought for fire at Colfax landmark

By Frank Oliver/Journal and Courier

VIEW FROM ABOVE: The destruction is evident when viewed from the top of a ladder truck on Thursday at the site of the former Miller's Fish Suppers restaurant in Colfax. One firefighter was slightly injured in the Wednesday blaze.

Officials say blaze may have started on ground floor, hope to pinpoint cause

By Joe Gerrety
Journal and Courier

COLFAX — Fire investigators hope to make a de-

Chief Brad Runk, still bleary-eyed from about 12 hours of work that continued through midnight

tell yet."

Investigators Thursday morning were still waiting for the arrival of the build-

Colfax blaze

Investigators are still trying to determine the cause of the fire that swept through Miller's Fish Suppers, destroying the one-time landmark.

The end of Miller's. December 13, 2000

One Colfax resident bemoaned how detached the town's people had become from each other. "You can't get people together to do anything like twenty years ago," he said. He added, "I sure miss all the hustle and bustle that went on in this town on a Saturday night." He was one of the handful of residents who attributed the fall of Miller's to its changeover from father to son. There are others in Colfax who point to the internal transition of the business' management as the root of the decline in customer numbers. Yet the numbers refute the accusation—Miller's enjoyed fifteen years of business that was its largest ever. Momentum might have sustained the business for a year or two after the transition in family management, but not for the fifteen years from 1972 to 1987. When pressed, those who pointed to the family management change will admit that the sale of the business to an outsider had been the fatal move.

Denizens of Colfax are left to debate whether Miller's would have eventually closed even if it had remained under the ownership of the Miller family. If the numbers had continued to ebb it's likely Mike Miller would have come to the same decision as Dan Furry. However, if the restaurant had closed while still owned by the Miller family, it would have closed doing things the "Miller way"—clean grease, impeccable quality, hospital-like cleanliness and a fanatic dedication to customer service; the business would not have been abandoned as a filthy, cockroach-infested shell.

Finally, there are some who feel inflexibility by the Millers in responding to a changing market led to the decline in their business. While possibly true, it was virtually impossible to alter a business philosophy that had been ingrained for nearly fifty years; a philosophy that found itself at odds with an evolving customer base. Catfish in the '90s actually became a "designer dish" on many restaurant menus. With the proliferation of pond-raised catfish, previous attitudes about it began to change. Chefs discovered the pleasingly mild flavor and texture of catfish and began inventing a wide range of methods for preparing the "whiskered walleye". Catfish was appearing on menus sauteed, broiled, baked, in soups, just about any way that fish could be prepared; it was no longer relegated to just being coated and plunged into cooking oil. The Miller's might have been able to expand their menu to include a wider range of catfish dishes, but not without a significant retooling of their kitchens. It would have been a significant risk, a risk that might not have dealt with the real issue of declining customer counts; the romance of a little out-of-the-way place in Colfax was no longer romantic—it was now just inconvenient.

Today, many people appear to no longer care if owners participate in the daily management of the business, an attitude that may have evolved because it's so rare to find a restaurant where the owners work as hard as the Millers to build relationships with their customers. In this day where many seem to have difficulty establishing personal relationships with anyone, the Miller's style may today actually appear intrusive to many.

All of the Miller family shrugs off the excruciatingly hard work that was invested in their business; after all, it's rare to find a restaurant manager today whose weekly schedule includes working six days of full shifts and then spending his or her seventh day cleaning the restaurant and waxing its floors as Jr. Miller did every week and then his son after him. Rather, the Millers continue to point to how much fun it was to be part of the business. A compromise and, in their minds, a deterioration toward modern-day restaurant standards would have not have been worth the trade.

Chapter Nine

"Our success came in a different time."

Jr. Miller continues to dream about his business. He often awakes after dreaming of a hard night's work behind the fryers; dreams that are often so vivid he finds himself as exhausted as if he'd put in one of his typical 18-hour days. After investing nearly 50 years in nurturing his business, it's not surprising he still dreams of what for him became a dream come true. He's tortured every morning as he sits at the kitchen table of the home he and Mary Ellen Miller have shared for over fifty years. He has an unobstructed view of the burned-out shell of the building that once housed the business that defined his life. His sadness at the sight of the decaying building is shared by many residents of Colfax who see the demise of Miller's as a stark symbol of the town's slide into obscurity. Most in Colfax reveled in the notoriety Miller's brought to the little town that until 1946 had only been known for being named for a former Vice President; few seem to mind that a catfish replaced Schuyler Colfax.

It's debatable if anyone could ever again realize such a dream in this day of commissary-based corporate cuisine or in such a remote place as Colfax. Jr. Miller is doubtful that even he could recreate his story in today's competitive environment and changing tastes, "People have to understand that our success came in a different time." Miller's stands as an anachronism in today's restaurant world and, if places like Miller's still exist, it's most likely they are owned and managed by the descendants of its founder. It would also be rare that any restaurant could find itself with a staff that would include the likes of Stella Bowen and the many others who gave decades of unwavering loyalty to the Miller family business. For the most part, today's restaurants are staffed with transients; few look at table

159

service as a noble career option. For those who do, they are keenly aware that competition for their services is intense and they are in a seller's market. If terminated from one job, they know it is likely they can procure new employment within 24 hours.

Whatever a person wants to call him—James, Jerry or Junior—he, his wife, son and daughter-in-law know one clear matter of fact—they made the dream a reality. It was a dream that had not been so vast to include having their family name become known across the nation, it just turned out that way. James L. Miller's humility would never allow him to consider himself alongside other Indiana business legends, but many of his former customers would be quick to nominate him for such distinction.

On June 4, 1996 James L. Miller faced the reality that he was about to die. He had been hospitalized for 18 days at Lafayette's Home Hospital with a mysterious illness physicians had been unable to diagnose and consequently been unable to treat. He had not been told he was near death, but he sensed it nearing. "They'd moved me to a dying room—you know— the double room where you're in bed in one room and the second room's for your family to sit around waiting for you to die." Mary Ellen Miller inadvertently discovered the prospect of her husband's death after overhearing a conversation between a doctor and a nurse. The sense of impending death brought him to thoughts of James O. and Anna May Miller and the path he had traveled over his own lifetime. In his prayers he asked the Lord for his forgiveness and reconciliation with his parents. Jr. Miller had earlier reconciled with his son, and now, assuming himself to be on the brink of death, he sought peace with his parents. His innate belief in a forgiving God that had led him to promise to never do business on Sunday now impelled him to seek the peace that would come from his parents' forgiveness.

Though his childhood bible teachings made Jr. Miller look at himself as a prodigal son returning to seek atonement through the forgiveness of his father, he is as much akin to a character from a Horatio Alger story. Unlike the prodigal son who left his father with the "portion of goods that falleth to me", Jr. Miller was a man of humble origin who traveled into the world with only his intelligence, vision and grit. He attributes much of his success to luck, but as an old saying goes, "The harder you work, the luckier you get." It was also fortuitous that Jr. Miller combined immense talent and iron-willed discipline with his hard work. To that end, he became one of the luckiest men in the world. Jr. Miller was released from the hospital on June 10, 1996 and has not consumed a drop of liquor since the day he entered the hospital; he celebrated his 83rd birthday on February 2, 2002.

That Jr. Miller would harbor regrets about his life is ironic. He freely admits to a life of heavy drinking and, although he was defending his property, he had shot and nearly killed a man. He had also owned a business that in its beginning epitomized everything his parents abhorred. But he worked tirelessly from the moment he purchased his business to transform it into a place that would soon earn a reputation as a place where families, more than anyone, were made to feel welcome and safe. A minister who often frequented the restaurant once told Jr. he brought his family to Colfax because he knew, "It's a place where my family is welcomed and treated with respect." Miller's evolved to where alcohol became an insignificant part of its business. By the early '70s, the counter of the bar area had been reduced to only five stools, which were most often used by people waiting for a table. Jr. Miller achieved his goal: he transformed the grimy tavern that served food, into a family restaurant where you could buy a drink if you wanted it. In the end, James O. and Anna May Miller would probably have been proud of their youngest son.

As to the question that a story like Miller's could be recreated today, some think a business like Miller's might succeed in a high traffic location in some large city. Rick Albrecht thinks a Miller's could be successful in the right location in Indianapolis if, as he says, "They operated like the old Miller's. The good food combined with their marvelous service would be a hit. But Colfax? It just couldn't happen today." Albrecht also believes that today's emphasis on theme and decor (something Miller's was never noted for) plays as significant a role in attracting customers as the food, "It's as much about show business as it is the menu."

Reid Duffy, noted Indiana restaurant critic and author of *Indiana's Favorite Restaurants* (Indiana University Press, 2002), takes the opposite side of the issue. "I feel that restaurant ownership is one of the last opportunities for the entrepreneur to successfully go head-to-head with the big guy." Duffy believes a well-managed restaurant could thrive in a small town. "The basic draw is still good food and good service. People seem to still like discovering good places to eat in little out-of-the-way places like Colfax." However, Duffy is skeptical that the Miller's menu of deep-fried foods could hold up in the face of today's health consciousness.

National chain restaurants have played a role in customer behavior by creating a "sense of sameness". While travelers used to seek out the best locally owned restaurants, they now seek the security of knowing that a restaurant will be, "Just like the one we have back home." It's an attitude that saw Miller's customer counts beginning to dwindle during the month of May as people frequented national chains in Indianapolis rather than traveling to Colfax.

For many, going to Miller's in a large city would just not be the same. Part of its mystique was the discovery of a special place tucked away in the remote cornfields of Clinton County, Indiana; as Johnny Rutherford said, "It was just a special place." Though the restaurant closed in August 1999, people from outside the local community still travel to Colfax, unaware that their cravings will go unsatisfied. They often stop by the Chatterbox Cafe, which occupies the old Cessna's Drugstore a block from Miller's front door, seeking information about Miller's. Owner Linda Phebus says some who inquire about Miller's are often visibly upset after hearing the sad details of the restaurant's final months. "There are a lot of people who have special memories of coming to Miller's—of coming to Colfax. When we tell them about what happened people sometimes react as though their family photo album had been burned up in that fire."

Of the many who contributed to the story of Miller's, Tom Cochrun, respected Indianapolis broadcast journalist and co-founder of Nineteenth Star, LLC, an Indianapolis-based media company, offered a succinct description of Colfax's most famous landmark.

"My mother and father were great fans of Miller's. Dad would always be excited when a trip was scheduled. I also learned to relish those trips, actually thinking about it days ahead. After my father passed away, we would return with Mom and so there were also great memories attached. We often visited with friends and the experience was always superb. The people were just great Hoosiers. The setting was a classic Midwest small town family restaurant that had a special charm. The food of course was unique and justified any craving we might have. Delicious. I've traveled a great deal and, as authentic, unique and good as some places are, I've never found a place quite like Miller's. It was a state of mind and sense of presence as well as great eating."

Tom Cochrun's recollection of Miller's might help many of us who call Indiana home to understand why we often struggle when asked, "What is a Hoosier?" We usually attempt to personify the term, when a place like

Miller's points to the possibility that a Hoosier is not a person at all, but actually an attitude—a state of mind. Miller's was as much a state of mind as it was a place. Many of the five million who traveled to Colfax would no doubt agree.

Mary Ellen and James L. Miller. June 29, 2001

Chapter Ten

The Employees

According to Mary Ellen Miller, "There are simply too many stories to tell about the wonderful people who helped us build a business. They weren't just employees—they were our friends, they were like our family." However difficult, an attempt is made here to acknowledge as many of the former Miller's staff who could be remembered or documented and served from October 1946 to April 1995. It's hoped that most who are included here have fond memories of their time at Miller's. In some cases, maiden names are used, married names in others, former married names in a few cases and, former, former married names in one or two others. There may be duplicates where someone is listed with both their maiden and married names. There may be some misspellings—it was thought to be more important to include the staff member even if the exact spelling of their name couldn't be confirmed. Unfortunately some may have been inadvertently omitted—it was not intentional; but business records and more often, memories sometimes fade. Five years of employment records (1956-1960) were destroyed in the 1980 fire that ravaged Miller's.

In the very beginning, October 21, 1946:

Stella Bowen	Betty Ann Ferguson	Don Ferguson
Iva Jackson	Bob Saunders	Raleigh Waggoner

And, the valued many who followed:

A

Charlotte Abbott
Julia Alexander
Steven Alexander
Patricia Ames
Glenda Anderson
Stephanie Anderson
Irene Ashley
Gloria Avery

Clyde Alexander
Patricia Alexander
Ted Alexander
Jo Ann Amick
Joan Anderson
Virginia Anderson
Ralph Ashley

Jerry Alexander
Susan Alexander
Tom Alexander
Ethel Anderson
Patricia Anderson
Celina Arroyo
Ruth Athey

B

Charlotte Bailey
Terry Baker
Jennifer Baugh
Suilon Benjamin
Charlene Blake
Martha Boggs
Betty Bowles
Tamatha Bowman
Thomas R. Boyles
Randy Bragg
John Bruning, Jr.
Elizabeth Bryant
Harry Bundy
Sherrill Burgun

Terry Bailey
Lola Barkley
Gordon Baumgardt
Bernice Birge
Terri Blacker
Julia Boling
Tamatha Bowen
E. David Boyles
Edgar Bradbury
Mary Brubaker
Valada Bruning
Addie Maud Bundy
May Bundy
Joyce Burnett

Betty J. Baker
Marcia Barnaby
Sherry Benge
Larry Birge
Barbara Boggs
Phyllis Bouldin
Tim Bowen
Molly Boyles
Phillip Bragg, Jr.
Shirley Breedlove
Clinton Bryant
Sarah Buedel
Pansy Bundy

C

Patsy Cain
Elizabeth Cash
Jo Ellen (Elliott) Clark
Gerry Clouser
Ora Coffman
Helen Boots Cook

Velera Cain
Louise Castle
Sue Clawson
Kevin Clouser
Sandra Colter
Janet Cook

Blanche Carson
Judy Catron
Elizabeth Clouser
Ruth Clouser
Gail Conwell
Lewis Cook

Tim Coridan
Miriam Crane
Maurice (Pat) Cripe
Carol Crull
Martha Cunningham

Richard Covault
Jessie Crews
Penny Cripe
Rita Crull
Penny Cunningham

Terry Cox
Beulah Cripe
Jean Crow
Kitty Cunningham

D

Avis Davis
J. Herron Davis
Mary Davis
Elaine Deen
Cindy Donoho
Bertha Dunwoody

Norma Davids
June Davis
Susie Davis
Lee Dobson
Nancy Dowell

Samuel Davidson
Marshall Davis
Winford C. Davis
Brenda Donoho
Linda Dye

E

Charlotte Eggers
Twalla Emery
Kelly Ezra

Jewell Emmitt
Kathryne Engle

Edith Emery
Teresa Ewing

F

A.J. Feltner
Ellen Feltner
Elizabeth Ferguson
Alice Fields
Glenda Ford

Alice Feltner
Susan Feltner
Howard Ferguson
Tracy Flack
Kathy Freels

David Feltner
Donald G. Ferguson
Madeline Ferguson
Joseph Flowers
Tim French

G

Linda Gillam
Clara Graves

James Goff
Carolyn Gross

Michelle Gramman

H

Dorothy Haag
Kim Haley
Jackie Hankins
Tadd Hankins
Michael Harlan
Viola Sue Harris
Bill Harrison
Sandra J. Hawkins
Diane Hill
Tim Hill
Linda Hise
Lera May Hodges
Wes Hodges
Anthony Houchens
Corey Houchens
Ross Howe
Charles W. Hunter

Tonya Haines
Linda (Blacker) Ham
Loyd Hankins
Denise Harlan
Mark Harlan
Anna May Harrison
Tammy Harvey
Jessica Herbert
Jim Hill
Lillie Ruth Hiner
Alyne Hodges
Penny Hodges
LaVaun Hoffman
Carolyn Houchens
David Houchens
Peggy Huffer

Ernest Haley
Devon Hankins
Lucille Hankins
Gaye Harlan
Robert Hardesty
Belva Harrison
Anthony Harvey
Raleigh Higer
Sharon Hill
Jim Hise
Deborah Hodges
Russ Hodges
Merle Hoffman
Christie Houchens
Mandy Howe
Denise Humphrey

I

Judith Imel

Mary Ingram

J

Lon Jackson

Clem Jenkins

Helen Johnson

K

Terri Jo Kahle
Jack Kauffman, Sr.
Mark Kauffman
Tony Kauffman
Evelyn Kennedy
Peggy Kincaid

Barbara Kauffman
Jack Kauffman, Jr.
Mary Kauffman
Tracey Kauffman
Ronald Kennedy
Dolly Kinslow

Dan Kauffman
Jerry Kauffman
Robert Kauffman
Charles Kelch
Jennery Key
Chad Kozuch

Scott Kozuch   Bernice Krolczyk

L

Clarence Laird   Linsey Laird   Kathy Lane
Georgia Lanum   Jackie Lanum   Lorran Lanum
Betty Lou Laverty   Ermadine Lawler   Mary P. Lease
Phyliss Leckrone   J.R. "Buck" Lenehan   Lorra Lenehan
Jeannette Leopard   Florence Lewis   Carolyn Sue Lind
Margaret Lind   Anna May Linedecker   Melvin Lockard
Lori Loveless

M

Ralph Maish   Pam Mandrell   Diana Marshall
Mary Marshall   Aaron Martin   Brianna Martin
Carolyn Martin   Krista Martin   Fred McBee
Colin McCarthy   Paul McCarthy   Sandra McKinsey
Tressie McKinsey   Thelma McMindes   Viola McKinsey
Twila Jo Melton   Joyce Merrill   Lola Miller
Peggy Sue Mills   Diana Mitchell   Darrell Moore
Grace Moore   Mary P. Moore   Patricia Moore
Kathy Morgan   Mary Morrison   Stanley Morrison
Tom Morrison   Barbara Morrow   Bernice Morrow
James Morrow   Theo Morrow   Earlene Murphy
Becky Myers   Emily Mullendore

N

Nancy Neff   Gerald Nelson   Anna Niebrand
Mary Lou Norton

O

James A. O'Connor   Debbie Ottinger

P

Rebecca Paddack	James B. Parke	Jeffrey Parke
Helen Payne	Michael Payne	Max Pendry
Debbie Perkins	Jenanette Perrin	Sue Perrin
Kathy Jo Peterson	Meda Phebus	Robert Phebus
Alma Pollett	Roberta Polley	Janice Poole
Pauline Potter	Judith Price	Connie Pritchard
Donald Pritchard	Naomi Puckett	Jacob Pulley

Q

Mary Quick

R

Janet Rabensteine	Edie Ritchart	Rick Ritchart
Helen Reinke	Barbara Revell	Dee Rhodes
James Rice	Judy Rice	Ruth Rice
Delores Riley	Charlotte Roberts	Deborah Roberts
Beatrice Robertson	Ermin A. Robertson	Ken Robertson
Scott Robey	Joe Robley, Sr.	Susie Rodgers
Orpha Rohler	Mary Rominger	Tammy Rominger
Eva Pearl Rose	Mary Lee Ross	

S

Kimberly Saari	Lutressie Selke	Patty Selke
Shirley Shahan	Cynthia Shelley	Johnny Shelley
Kristin Shelley	Johnny Shelley	Ryan Shelley
Lucy Shuler	Sally Skow	Dwight Slipher
Bettie Smith	Vernie Smart	Boston Smith
Christine Smith	Elaine Smith	R. Stephen Smith
Thomas K. Smith	Maragret Smock	Geri Snowden
Mildred Snowden	Eric Spencer	William Steele
Larry Southern	Pam Southern	Chas. Stambaugh
Nancy Steele	Diane Stewart	Marjorie Stingley

Deborah Stambaugh
Marvin Storm
Jamie Strong
Michelle Swafford

Karen Ann Stingley
Jimmy Street
Louise Suter
Pamela Swinford

Beverly Stockton
Saundra Street
Diane Swafford
Shannon Swilley

T

Bret Taylor
Alice Thomas
Altha Thomerson

Mary Taylor
Gladys Thomas
Carol Thomerson

Ann Thayer
Janet Thomas
Ellen Thornton

V

Kristie VanDeventer

Robin VanDeventer

Jacqueline Veruete

W

Francis Waggoner
Susan Walker
Elizabeth Walters
Patricia Walters

Virginia Waggoner
Anita Walters
Jeff Walters
Mary Margaret
Walton

Mary Walker
Betty Walters
Libbi Walters
Margaret Warren

Joy Watkins
Elizabeth Wells
Gregory White
Virginia White
Michael Wingate
Elizabeth Woods
Betty Wyant

Pearl Weller
Margaret Wells
Margaret White
David Williams
Ellen Witte
Matt Woods
John "Mr. Fix-It"
Walters

Ann Wells
Bruce Welshimer
Thelma White
Diane Williams
Maria Wood
Deborah Wortley

Y

Geraldine Young

Teresa Young

Scott Robey

Bibliography

Advertisement for J.H. Girt & Co. store. *Colfax Chronicle* (Colfax, Ind.), December 20, 1877, pg. 1.

Advertisement for Big 4 Restaurant, *The Colfax Standard* (Colfax, Ind.), June 24, 1905, pg. 1.

Earl Anderson advertisement for Crosely radios, *Clinton County Review* (Colfax, Ind.), January 6, 1927, pg. 5.

"Johns' Restaurant Sold", *Clinton County Review* (Colfax, Ind.), January 27, 1927, pg. 1.

"Brooks Sells Restaurant", *Clinton County Review*, (Colfax, Ind.), September 1, 1927, pg.1.

"Six Negroes Run Amok on Road 52 Saturday Night", *Clinton County Review* (Colfax, Ind.), November 6, 1930, pg. 1.

"Buys Thurman Restaurant", *Clinton County Review* (Colfax, Ind.), October 19, 1933, pg. 1.

"Hickory Inn Will Be Open Saturday Night", *Clinton County Review* (Colfax, Ind.), March 14, 1935, pg. 1.

"Purchases Store Building", *Clinton County Review* (Colfax, Ind.), January 7, 1937, pg. 1.

"Colfax Men Jailed Following Fracas", *Clinton County Review* (Colfax, Ind.), October 24, 1946, pg. 1.

Advertisement announcing catfish suppers served every night. *Clinton County Review* (Colfax, Ind.), January 16, 1947, pg. 7.

"Wesleyan Methodist Revival", *Clinton County Review* (Colfax, Ind.), May 22, 1947, pg. 1.

"Santa Will Visit With Youngsters", *Clinton County Review* (Colfax, Ind.), December 11, 1947, pg. 1.

"James Millers Entertain Employees Sun. Evening", *Clinton County Review* (Colfax, Ind.), December 2, 1948, pg. 1.

"James Brooks Purchases "400 Club" At Frankfort", *Clinton County Review* (Colfax, Ind.), February 5, 1948, pg. 1.

"Air Conditioning Added To Miller's Café", *Clinton County Review* (Colfax, Ind.), June 24, 1948, pg. 1.

"Miller's Expands Dining Room", *Clinton County Review* (Colfax, Ind.), March 10, 1949, pg. 7.

"Sour Grapes" On The Menu", *Clinton County Review* (Colfax, Ind.), April 6, 1950, pg. 1.

"Minstrel Show Ready For Curtain March 9", *Clinton County Review* (Colfax, Ind.), March 8, 1951, pg. 1.

Advertisement for Anderson Free Bean Supper, *Clinton County Review* (Colfax, Ind.), November 8, 1951, pg. 8.

Hillhouse Restaurant advertisement, *Clinton County Review* (Colfax, Ind.), June 27, 1952, pg. 10.

"184 Basketball Fans At Dinner", *Clinton County Review* (Colfax, Ind.), April 19, 1957, pg. 1.

Advertisement for Miller's Thanksgiving dinner. *Clinton County Review* (Colfax, Ind.), November 22, 1957 pg. 11.

Advertisement for Miller's Christmas dinner, *Clinton County Review* (Colfax, Ind.), December 20, 1957, pg. 7.

"Install Swimming Pool At Miller Home", *Clinton County Review*, (Colfax, Ind.) April 18, 1958. pg. 1.

"Italian Workmen And Citizens Clash At Colfax", *Frankfort Weekly Times* (Frankfort, Ind.), July 2, 1904 pg. 1.

"The Saloon Men (sic) On His Wagon", *Frankfort Daily Crescent* (Frankfort, Indiana) via the *Thorntown Enterprise* (Thorntown, Ind.), December 1, 1906 pg. 1.

James O. Miller death notice, *Frankfort Morning Times* (Frankfort, Ind.), September 15, 1932, pg. 1

James O. Miller obituary, *Frankfort Morning Times* (Frankfort, Ind.), October 2, 1932, pg. 1.

Anna May Miller death notice, *Frankfort Morning Times* (Frankfort, Ind.), July 28, 1936, pg. 1.

"Sgt. Frank A. Ashley Missing In Action Over Austria June 16", *Frankfort Morning Times* (Frankfort, Ind.), June 29, 1944, pg. 1.

"Frankfort Gunner Is Killed Over Austria", *Frankfort Morning Times* (Frankfort, Ind.), June 7, 1945, pg. 1.

Miller's first advertisement, *Frankfort Morning Times* (Frankfort, Ind.), November 24, 1946, pg. 6.

James Brooks obituary, *Frankfort Morning Times* (Frankfort, IN), September 20, 1962, pg. 1.

"Businessman hits ruling by Judge" *Frankfort Morning Times* (Frankfort, Ind.) April? 1971*.

"Billboard beef no fish story", *The Times* (Frankfort, IN), October 25, 1972, pg. 13.

"Fire's out, but Miller's isn't", *The Times* (Frankfort, IN), January 20, 1980, pg. 1.

"From fire back to the frying pan", *The Times* (Frankfort, IN), March 5, 1980, pg. 1.

"Miller's Restaurant closing", Derrick Gingery, *The Times*, Frankfort, IN, July 8, 1999, pg. 1.

"Miller's may not close." *The Times* (Frankfort, IN) July 16, 1999, pg. 1.

"Colfax restaurant not closing." *The Times* (Frankfort, IN), July 23, 1999, pg. 1.

"Miller's restaurant burns." *The Times* (Frankfort, IN), December 14, 2000, pg. 1.

"Residents remember county landmark", *The Times*, (Frankfort, IN), December 14, 2000, pg. 1.

"Restaurant fire investigated." *The Times* (Frankfort, IN), December 15, 2000, pg. 1.

"Restaurant fire ruled arson." *The Times* (Frankfort, IN), December 16, 2000, pg. 1.

"Restaurant arson stumps investigators." *The Times* (Frankfort, IN), December 13, 2001, pg. 1.

Table Talk, Marge Hanley, "Gone Fishin'", *Indianapolis News* (Indianapolis, IN), June 25, 1987*.

"If it's catfish you want, try Miller's", *Indianapolis Star* (Indianapolis, IN), August 10, 1986, pg. 21.

"Chains are eating up market share in city", *Indianapolis Star* (Indianapolis, IN), July 13, 2002, pgs. C1 & C3.

The World's a Stage, Henry Butler, *Indianapolis Times* (Indianapolis, Indiana), June 30, 1958*.

Graham Crackers, Gordon Graham, *Journal and Courier* (Lafayette, Ind.), March 11, 1957, pg. 18.

"Broncos Hang First Loss on Otterbein, Whip Colfax, 62-47", *Journal and Courier* (Lafayette, Ind.), March 11, 1957, pg. 18.

"Man shot, one held in Colfax break-in", *Journal and Courier* (Lafayette, IN), May 10, 1967*.

"Colfax could be spelled M-i-l-l-e-r-'-s", *Journal and Courier* (Lafayette, IN), February 18, 1979, pg. B-5*.

"Restaurateur Miller unpretentious, but how can he cook", *Journal and Courier* (Lafayette, IN), February 18, 1979, pg. B-8*.

"Fire ruins famed catfish site", *Journal and Courier* (Lafayette, IN), January 20, 1980, pg. 1.

Best Restaurants Poll, *Journal and Courier* (Lafayette, IN), February 20, 1983, pg. D-1

The Best Country Restaurants", *Journal and Courier* (Lafayette, IN), August 9, 1987, pg. C-1

"Answers sought for fire at Colfax landmark." *Journal and Courier* (Lafayette, IN), December 15, 2000. pg. 1.

"Colfax fire ruled an arson", *Journal and Courier* (Lafayette, IN), December 16, 2000. pg. 1.

"Catfish-Town, USA", *Gazette-Times* (Corvallis, Oregon) September 4, 1976*

Deborah Paul, *"Holy Catfish"*, *Indianapolis Monthly*, August 1983, pg. 81

Midwest Living (Meredith Publishing, Des Moines, Iowa) 4/87. Pg. 122. *

Clayburgh, Hon. Joseph. *History of Clinton County, Indiana*, A.W.Bowen & Co., Indianapolis, Indiana 1913

Crawford, Linda. *The Catfish Book*, University Press of Mississippi, 1991

Smith, Willard H., *SCHUYLER COLFAX: The Changing Fortunes of a Political Idol*. Indiana Historical Press, Indianapolis, Indiana. 1952.

Twain, Mark. *Mississippi Writings*, New York: Literary Classics of American, 1982.

Frankfort City Directory, R.L. Polk & Co. Publishers, Indianapolis, Indiana 1937-38 and 1948

City Directory of Frankfort, Indiana 1935. The Hoffman Directories, Quincy, Illinois

The Holy Bible, King James Version. The World Publishing Co. Cleveland, Ohio

1994-95 Membership Directory; Restaurant & Hospitality Association of Indiana; Indianapolis, IN

Office of the Recorder, Clinton County, Indiana

Office of the Surveyor, Clinton County, Indiana

"Earl Anderson: Colfax Businessman 1899-1985", Earl Anderson biography. Unknown author. Colfax Public Library.

Planet Catfish. www.planetcatfish.com

Ed Reiter's Color Television History. www.novia.net/~ereitan

Miller's Restaurant daily business logs and records.

Miller family archive of photography, clippings, and customer and other correspondence.*

*Clipping from Miller's archives, some exact dates and page numbers omitted.

Photography Credits

All photography was taken from the Miller family archive with the following exceptions:

Pages 3 and 44.   Courtesy of Mr. LeRoy Good.

Pages 99 and 100.   Courtesy of Mrs. Betty Grim.

Page 155.   Printed with permission from the *Journal and Courier*, Lafayette, Indiana. Article written by Mr. Joe Gerrety, photography by Mr. Frank Oliver.

About the Author.

Scott Robey is a native of Colfax, Indiana. He has spent most of his professional career in advertising and public relations. He has worked as an independent marketing services consultant since 1996.

As was the case with many teenage boys growing up in Colfax, Robey worked as a bus boy at Miller's Restaurant. He has been a close friend of the Miller family for nearly fifty years. Robey and his beautiful wife, Susan, live in Lafayette, Indiana.

Printed in the United States
1346300003B/85